PENGUIN BOOKS

*Letters to Sherlock Holmes*

# LETTERS TO Sherlock Holmes

SELECTED BY
RICHARD LANCELYN GREEN

PENGUIN BOOKS

Penguin Books Ltd, Harmondsworth, Middlesex, England
Viking Penguin Inc., 40 West 23rd Street, New York, New York 10010, U.S.A.
Penguin Books Australia Ltd, Ringwood, Victoria, Australia
Penguin Books Canada Ltd, 2801 John Street, Markham, Ontario, Canada L3R 1B4
Penguin Books (N.Z.) Ltd, 182–190 Wairau Road, Auckland 10, New Zealand

First published 1985

Made and printed in Great Britain by
Richard Clay (The Chaucer Press) Ltd,
Bungay, Suffolk
Filmset in 10/13pt Monophoto Photina by
Northumberland Press Ltd, Gateshead,
Tyne and Wear

# Contents

Letter from the Secretary to Sherlock Holmes     7

Foreword     9

*Part One: Early Correspondence*

*Part Two: From the Abbey House Archives*

*Part Three: Current Correspondence*

1. Mr Sherlock Holmes     45
2. Friends and Associates     105
3. Collectors     122
4. Professional Inquiries     133
5. Case Histories     147
6. The Supernatural     177
7. Personal Problems and Riddles     188
8. 221B Baker Street     196
9. Sherlockian Institutions     207
10. Letters about the Letters     219
    How Mr Holmes's Secretaries Replied     231

Dear Reader,

Letters addressed to Sherlock Holmes have been answered by the staff of the Abbey National Building Society for over fifty years and I am the latest to serve as his secretary.

The head office, Abbey House, stands in Baker Street and includes the number 221 which many would say is the site of the rooms which Holmes shared with Dr Watson. The present building was opened in 1932 as the headquarters of what was then the Abbey Road Building Society, but which in 1944 took its present name following the merger with the National Building Society. In 1951 it housed the Sherlock Holmes Exhibition which was arranged by the St Marylebone Public Library as a contribution to the Festival of Britain. The Exhibition included a reconstruction of the famous sitting-room, which won wide acclaim, being visited by over half a million people, including Queen Mary.

Letters still arrive in large quantities, and during my time in office, Mr Holmes has received post from every quarter of the globe. There are fan letters, birthday wishes, Christmas cards (one each year is from Dr Watson), invitations to give lectures or attend weddings. Sometimes he learns that he is the potential winner of a fortune or that he has been specially selected to receive a trial subscription to a well-known periodical, but by far the largest number of letters contain details of intriguing mysteries. He is asked to trace, as it may be, a peanut thief in Kansas or to bring to justice the chopstick murderer of Nagasaki or to end the nuclear arms race. A few bring news of Professor Moriarty some claiming that he has been spotted boarding a train in Neasden or that he is responsible for the theft of a painting from the Dulwich Gallery. Others again wish to know intimate details of the detective's private life. Was he left- or right-handed? Did he dislike gooseberry jam? Did he once wound Mrs Hudson in the foot while cleaning a revolver? And did Mycroft Holmes wear glasses?

These and other questions are hard to answer, and I have to remind his correspondents that Holmes is now spending much of his time in Sussex and is rarely, if ever, on hand to deal with the queries himself. But I know that he appreciates all the kind comments made about him and is touched by the evidence of the high regard in which he is held.

He will always reside at 221B Baker Street, but if the Abbey National Building Society has been able to play its part in sustaining his tenancy then that is a cause for satisfaction. I certainly enjoy the work and could not wish for a better or more distinguished employer.

Best wishes.

Yours faithfully

Sue Brown
Secretary to Sherlock Holmes

SB:VC

# Foreword

Sherlock Holmes has been receiving letters since 1890 when a tobacconist in Philadelphia wrote for a copy of his monograph on tobacco ash. Requests then came thick and fast from all over the world, for autographs, photographs, for immediate assistance in dealing with bizarre mysteries, and even for a lock of his hair. Sir Arthur Conan Doyle was the chief recipient, but letters also found their way to various addresses in Baker Street, to Scotland Yard, and to people such as Dr Joseph Bell or William Gillette who shared certain attributes of the great detective. Few unfortunately survive. Those in the early section of this book date from the time of Holmes's retirement, along with others which Conan Doyle mentioned in an article about Sherlock Holmes in the *Strand Magazine* in 1917 and which he placed in the same category.

Although the interior became familiar, the exact location of 221B Baker Street was and remains a matter for debate. In 1921 Dr Gray Chandler Briggs decided that it must be at 111 as this was opposite Camden House which is the name of the 'Empty House' from which Holmes and Watson could see into their sitting-room. By 1933 his theory had gained wide acceptance, but also by then the upper part of the street had been incorporated into Baker Street creating a real postal address at 221, part of the new Abbey House. Letters arrived at both addresses. The first known to have been received by the Abbey Road Building Society was in 1935, and there was considerable publicity about another, two years later, which was delivered to British Home Stores who had an office in the same building. More undoubtedly followed with Abbey House gaining total ascendancy following the destruction of 111 during the Blitz.

In 1949 Michael Hall became the first new tenant at 221B, as this was used as the official address for the *London Mystery Magazine* and his right to do so was upheld when contested in court by Conan Doyle's eldest son. The publicity accompanying the launch of the periodical led to a flood of letters with many addressed to the original tenant. More followed in 1950 when the St Marylebone Public Library announced its plan for a Sherlock Holmes exhibition. Many of Holmes's friends then wrote to the papers or to him personally offering objects for display, and others wrote later to congratulate him upon the result. They were answered by the librarian.

After the exhibition, the post was filled by John Greaves of the Abbey National. Although not the first 'stand-in' for Sherlock Holmes, as his predecesor Samuel Morton had dealt with earlier letters, Greaves was in many ways the best-suited to the job being an enthusiastic Sherlockian and the Secretary of the Dickens Fellowship. Knowing the stories by heart and having the benefit of the recent exhibition, he could speak with authority on the subject. When asked, for example, to explain the disappearance of a frogman, he suggested that the Lion's Mane may have been responsible. He also had cards printed to be sent to the correspondents, one of Sherlock Holmes and one of his sitting-room, and later there was a pamphlet entitled 'The Immortal Sherlock Holmes'. Since his time there have been a number of secretaries, including Jill Nicholson, Lesley Whitson and Chris Bazlinton. Although appointed blind without necessarily having even read the stories, each has sustained the correspondence in an admirable way with great common sense and good humour.

Newspapers, periodicals, television and school textbooks frequently remind the reading and non-reading public of the delightful fact that they can indulge in the ultimate whimsy and make known their admiration for Sherlock Holmes by writing to him direct and in the certain knowledge that a reply will be sent on his behalf. Letters from the most eminent Sherlockian scholars are perhaps sent to his secret address in Sussex, but those which arrive in London are by no means unworthy of their subject.

In making this selection, thanks are due to the Sir Arthur Conan Doyle Foundation in Lausanne for permission to include the early letters and those received at the Château de Lucens (where there is also a reconstruction of Holmes's sitting-room); to the Abbey National Building Society for the use of all the remaining letters and for their help in compiling this book; and, of course, to the correspondents themselves. The book is intended as a tribute to Arthur Conan Doyle and should provide confirmation, if such were needed, that to the world at large Sherlock Holmes is still *the* detective. He has seldom been referred to in any other way for he eclipses and predominates the whole of his profession.

## PART ONE

*Early Correspondence*

## A Bee-Keeper's Offer of Assistance

10 October 1904

W.B.C. Apiary
Old Bedford Road
Luton, Beds.

Dear Sir,

I see by some of the morning papers that you are about to retire and take up beekeeping. I know not if this be correct or otherwise, but if correct I shall be pleased to render you service by giving any advice you may require.

I make this offer in return for the pleasure your writings gave me as a youngster, they enabled me to spend many and many a happy hour. Therefore I trust you will read this letter in the same spirit that it is written.

Yours respectfully,
W. Herrod


## A Housekeeper for Sherlock Holmes

10 October 1904

c/o The Hon. P. Cranstoun
Hurst Hill House
Totland Bay, Isle of Wight

To Sir Conan Doyle, Bart,

Will 'Mr Sherlock Holmes' require a housekeeper for his country cottage at Xmas? I know someone, who loves a quiet country life, and 'Bees' especially, an old-fashioned quiet woman.

Yours faithfully,
M. Gunton

# Request for an Autograph

*18 November 1904*                    *9 Eriswell Road, Worthing*

Dear Sir,

I trust I am not trespassing too much on your time and kindness by asking for the favour of your autograph to add to my collection.

I have derived very much pleasure from reading your Memoirs, and should very highly value the possession of your famous signature.

Trusting you will see your way to thus honour me, and venturing to thank you very much in anticipation,

    I am, Sir, Your obedient Servant,
                    Charles Wright

P.S. Not being aware of your present address, I am taking the liberty of sending this letter to Sir A. Conan Doyle, asking him to be good enough to forward it to you.

Sherlock Holmes Esq.


# A Letter of Appreciation

*10 June 1910*                              *New York, USA*

Dear Mr Holmes,

I have read with great interest the reminiscences of your detective achievements, as recorded by your friend, John H. Watson, M.D. I would like you to know how greatly I admire your skill in every way; but especially in that great case which goes by the name of *The Hound of the Baskervilles*. Might I ask you, as a special favour to myself, to send me your autograph? You cannot think how delighted I would be to add it to my collection!

    Yours faithfully,
      *Etc.*

# Letters to Conan Doyle

## The Revival of Sherlock Holmes

29 August 1897                                    Baltimore, Maryland, USA

Dear Sir,

We, being ardent admirers of your famous works, write to ask if you will favour us with another one of your works on the famous detective Sherlock Holmes, thereby favouring not only us, but the world's public.

> Yours respectfully,
> > C. V. Rice, B. Tyker, M. Mullins

Dr A. Conan Doyle


## Letter from a Russian Girl*

28 June 1904                                    Rajgrod, Lomzer Guber.
                                                Russ., Polen

To Sir Arthur Conan Doyle

Dear Lord,

Your world-renowned work made on me a very great impression. I am not rich, I beg a charity, do if you please send me your work or in English or German or Russian languages. I am a great lover of it, my whole time is only in science and reading, but I am in a little village place where I can not get and there is no library whatever, therefore I beg if you please to be so kind and oblige me with your work and forever will bless you.

> Your humble servant and admirer,
> > Simeon Grajevsky

*\* Signed as if from her father*

# The Little Russian Girl, Again

*21 April* ·               *Rajgrod, Lomzer Guber.*
                               *Russ., Polen*

To Sir Arthur Conan Doyle

Dear Lord!

I beg if you please, I am a little girl thirteen years of age and I admire much your writing, I am quite excited; I did read a few in the Russian language. I know the English language a little and I asked Papa to buy for me your work in the original English language, but he says he can't afford it, he has better to keep up his poor family, and he is not rich, so I beg of you Dear and noble Lord, do if you please send me your work, if not all of them, yet a few of them. I will forever thank you and it will be a surprise to Dear Papa, as it will come to his address. Papa also knows well the English language, you will make happy me poor little girl, who admires and loves you very much.

    Your little humble servant, awaiting the books,

                                      Rebekka Grajewski

# The Grosvenor Treasure Chart

*10 March 1905*           *P.O. Box 777, 19, Hampson's Buildings,*
                       *Smith Street, Durban, South Africa*

Sir Conan Doyle

Sir,

Knowing the interest you take in cipher codes, I take the liberty of writing you on the subject.

    I enclose a chart procured from either the Admiralty, or their Cape Town agents, or else the Cape Archives, I am not sure which. The history is as follows:

    The *Grosvenor*, an Indiaman, was wrecked on the coast of Pondoland, about 150 miles south of here, in, I think, 1782. As passengers

she carried the India officers and treasure from the sack of Delhi. The latter being the Crown Jewels, etc., and gold coin. The exact spot of the wreck is known – the cannon being lodged in the rocks on the spot. The people landed, bringing with them one case which probably contained the jewels. All the remaining cases were left on board and, as these contained gold coinage, the deduction is that the one brought on shore contained something even more valuable, i.e. jewellery. To this day, after a big storm, gold coins are washed ashore and stick in the fissures of the rocks. Many have been brought to Durban and sold. Some dating back 2,000 years to the first king of Delhi.

The Pondo legend says that the one case was taken by a party of officers up a certain valley at sunset. They could not have proceeded far as they were all in camp, asleep, by daylight. They then made the great mistake of setting off overland to Cape Town, although they had carpenters, tools and material for building boats. All the men and officers were killed with the exception of four sailors who arrived, with a chart of the buried treasure, at Cape Town after much hardship. The ladies were taken prisoner by the Pondos, and their descendants are there to this day. On the chart arriving at London the Admiralty – together with the only key to the cipher – was burned down. It appears that in those days each Indiaman had her own private code of semaphore signals as, being at war with France, it was considered better that they should not be acquainted with all signals by capturing one vessel. Three-armed semaphores were then used.

It is therefore to be believed that the case contained the Royal Jewels and that same is still undiscovered.

I believe that very few people are aware of the above facts, but a few Johannesburg people propose a small syndicate to cover expenses of an expedition to hunt for the treasure. If a man wanted to bury a chest he would naturally choose some spot where some natural prominency, such as a big rock, would be easily indicated in a chart. I suppose that the expedition will work from that point of view.

The syndicate is being kept secret for the present, I believe, so kindly treat this as confidential.

Both the ciphers and their keys will no doubt be procurable in London, belonging to other ships of the same date, which might be of service in deciphering the enclosed chart. The 'X' evidently represents the spot of burial, and the semi-circle may represent a line of quartz or rock, or possibly a line of bush-edge.

I should be glad to hear your opinion as to the possibility of deciphering this and beg to remain, Sir,

Yours faithfully,
R. G. Pearson

## A Polish Murder Trial

*19 October 1913*                                                    *Warsaw*

Dear Sir,

Having been for many years one of your constant and appreciative readers is the only excuse I can make in addressing you, being as I am a perfect stranger and a foreigner. There is shortly going to take place in Warsaw what promises to be one of the most sensational murder trials yet known there. The murdered man, Prince Lubecki, and the supposed murderer, his friend Monsieur de Bisping, are well known in Warsaw Society. Bisping protests his innocence and all who know him think it impossible he could be capable of committing such a crime. However, up to now there seem to be many incriminating circumstances and no other murderer or suspected person has been found.

It is to solve this mystery that I allow myself to approach you. Would you go to Warsaw and give your valuable help and advice to Mr de Bisping's lawyer – I may be quite wrong in supposing that you undertake such investigations, but in the event of your being kindly willing to help to unravel this mystery, would you be good enough to say at what fee? The same to include all travelling and hotel expenses. I have not yet approached the Bisping family with any suggestion of your aid, but in the event of your answer being in the affirmative I would at once write to them. Your name and writings are so well known all over Russia and Poland that I feel certain your advice would meet with the fullest appreciation. With many apologies for taking the liberty of addressing you, permit me to sign myself one of your great admirers,

Félix de Halpert

## PART TWO

# From the Abbey House Archives

## Sherlock Holmes in Indiana

*December 1954*                                        *Indianapolis, Indiana, USA*

Dear Sherlock Holmes,

When I go to Europe, I want to see your house on Baker Street. My father read me 'The Speckled Band', 'The Six Napoleons', and 'The Red-Headed League'. I hope he reads me more. You're quite clever at solving cases. When I grow up, I'm going to belong to the 'Sherlock Holmes Club'. I read about you in the comics, in the newspapers, too. My sister and I play 'Sherlock Holmes', but I have to be Watson. We have two long-haired dachounds [*sic*] and when we play 'Sherlock Holmes', we pretend that they are bloodhounds. A magazine said you went to Indiana, USA. Did you?

Sincerely,
> Betsy Rosasco


## Greetings from Denmark

*30 December 1954*                                        *Copenhagen, Denmark*

Dear Mr Holmes,

May I first of all congratulate you with your 100 years' birthday this year, I hope you are getting on well in spite of your great age. The reason why I write is that I am very interested in all things concerning you, and I already have a small collection of pictures, press-cuttings, etc. The only thing which I am short of is a picture of you, and – if you will be so kind – signed.

You see, I have several times here in Denmark tried to get hold of such a picture, but in vain, and therefore I try the last resource, to ask you.

Hoping that I do not give you any trouble, and waiting for your kind reply, I remain,

Yours faithfully,
> Flemming Møller

# Crimes of Passion

*Berlin-Dahlem, West Germany*

Dear Sir,

Being an enthusiastic reader of your adventures, I would beg you for
an answer. How much is love root of crimes? Is it really possible to
become a criminal because of love?

I thank you just now for your answer.

Hans Rauschning


# Basil Rathbone

*13 November 1955*                          *Columbus, Ohio, USA*

Dear Mr Holmes,

I am writing to you in the hope that you can locate a certain actor,
Basil Rathbone. Since he is of English birth, I thought you might be
interested in the case. I am trying to locate him because of the excellent
job he did in portraying you in several motion pictures.

Also, say hello to your housekeeper, Mrs Hudson, your brother
Mycroft, Inspector Lestrade and, of course, good old Watson. Oh, yes,
and Moriarty too, if you should happen to run over – oops! – into him.
Thank you.

Yours truly, your American friend,

Charles M. Pickard, and his
friend, Thomas F. Boldman

## A Popular Television Personality

*March 1956*                                    *Redcliffe, Iowa, USA*

Dear Mr Holmes,

Would you please give me some information on what I could do, while growing up, to become a better citizen. Would you suggest a book I could read? I would like to have this for English class.

I picked you because I have read some of the stories of you and I watch your television programme and I like it very much.

Could you please send me an autographed book or picture of you?

An admirer,
            Brian Keig

# The Marble
# and Cocoa Seed Offer
# from Ashanti

*9 April 1956*                          *Akumadan, Ashanti, Gold Coast*

My Dear Holmes,

I have much pleasure to inform you this my few lines. Dear Holmes, kindly send me some photographs of your own. How old are you? What class are you? And kindly send me some adventure comics and toys. If you send me all these things, I will send you my photographs and newspapers.

I know how to play a football very well, so if you have a football boot and story book about football, kindly send me some. If you send me all these things, I will send you some marbles and cocoa seeds.

If anybody writes you, do not give him or her reply because I want to take you only as my best friend in the world. So if anyone write you, simply tell him that I cannot take you as my best friend, because I am a friend of Samuel who is at Ashanti, Gold Coast.

Joy to send me your brothers' and your sisters' photographs and address. If you haven't any pair of boots, kindly send me some anklets. If you received this letter, write me by air mail. I will send you my brothers' and sisters' photographs if I receive your photographs. Greeting!

Yours faithfully,
Samuel K. Amoah

## The Brazilian Burglar Business

*15 April 1956*                                    *Joao Passoa, Paraiba, Brazil*

Mr Sherlock Holmes,

I was surprised to see your address in one of your books. You are well-known here for your famous detective novels. Who does not admire the man who discovered that the man was a cobbler and left-handed solely from the dirty part of his breeches?

What I am going to ask for is a very simple thing. I would like to receive a photograph of you, autographed if possible, to hang up in a room of my house. I am sure that if some burglar tries to enter my house and sees your photograph on the wall he will never dare to break in again. That is all I want from the greatest detective in the world.

I think you must have retired, have you not? Since your adventures took place a long time ago, I think you must be very old. Anyhow, long live the greatest detective the world has ever had!

Yours,
Heitor Cabral da Silva

[From the Portuguese]

# The Mysterious Disappearance
## of Commander Crabb

22 May 1956                                    Hamburg, West Germany

Dear Sherlock Holmes!

You are one of the most prominent detectives of the world. It's known notorious that you have dissolved the heaviest criminal affairs on your writing-table. Now I would enjoy very much to hear your opinion about the disappearance of the frogman Crabb. Please answer me, if it's possible.

Your
    Heino Karkutsch

Would you mind sending me a signed photo of you, for I'm eager to see how you look like.

# The Adventures of Dermot Briant,
## Investigator

September 1956                           Ferry Hotel, Littlestone-on-Sea,
                                        New Romney, Kent

Dear Mr Holmes,

I have always been very interested in your cases and the way you deduce things. Could you deduce, for instance, anything about me from this letter? I am sure you could. I practise at deducing things. You can find out a lot at a hotel without anyone knowing. A few discreet inquiries at the receptionist and a look at the Visitors' Book tells me anyone's name, nationality, address, car number, room number and how long they are staying.

If you have some spare time, instead of taking cocaine or driving poor Dr Watson mad by shooting holes in the wall, I would be very grateful if you could write to me and give me a few hints on observation, but not if you prefer the cocaine.

Please give my regards to your brother Mycroft and Dr Watson.

Yours sincerely,
Dermot Briant
P.S. I will be here till the 8th of September.

## The Detection of Crime

*8 September 1956*                              *Passaic, New Jersey, USA*

Mr Holmes,

Would you rather use the old time means of law detection or the modern means?
Please send me an acknowledgement.

Yours truly,
T. Halatin

## The Delicate Matter of the Dutch Royal Family

*19 September 1956*                              *Edinburgh, Scotland*

Dear Mr Holmes,

I hear that you are very good in solving problems. Would you please try and solve mine. In 'A Case of Identity' you received a very beautiful jewelled ring. Please, what was the connection between the ring and the reigning family in Holland? I hope this does not put you to any trouble.

Would you also please send me a photograph of you and your sitting-room.

I do hope you will answer my problem.

Yours sincerely,
Helen McCabe

# The Freshman Class
## of Bacchus High School

*3 October 1956*                    *International Falls, Minnesota, USA*

Dear Mr Holmes,

We, the Freshman Class of Bacchus Junior High, have read your many interesting stories and were very surprised to see how you solved the many cases with your shrewdness. Since we have just finished reading one of your stories, 'The Adventure of the Speckled Band', we decided to write and ask you a few questions.

We would like to know what was the most difficult case you ever encountered? Has there ever been a case so baffling that you could not solve it? If so, what were the clues that misled you?

Thank you for your consideration,

Class Secretary

# The Black Pearl of the Borgias

*8 October 1956*                    *St Meinrad, Indiana, USA*

Dear Mr Holmes,

I have just finished reading your story, 'The Adventure of the Six Napoleons'. I liked the story very much and enjoyed the way you handled the case.

I should like it very much if you would send me a list of some of your other books, so I could read more of your exciting stories.

However, I would like to know one thing about the ending of the story of 'The Six Napoleons'. Did you return the black pearl that you found in the statue, or was it yours to keep since the preceding owner of the bust signed all the possible rights over to you?

Please answer soon.

An admirer of yours,

Robert Marks

## Moriarty in Damascus!

*26 October 1956*                    *American Embassy, USIS,*
                                          *Damascus, Syria*

Dear Sir,

I remember reading that Dr Moriarty died some years ago in Switzer-land. But only last night I was having a very quiet drink in Freddie's Bar in Damascus and a person arrived who introduced himself as the famous Dr Moriarty.

How can this be, and is my new friend an impostor?

Yours truly,
                    Hakki Nayal


## The Baker Street Show

*January 1957*                    *Chicago, Illinois, USA*

Dear Sherlock Holmes,

Did Dr Watson work with you on television?

If you have time, please answer my letter. Thank you, Mr Sherlock Holmes.

                                          J. D. Bartlett


## The Broadcasters of Brooklyn

*27 February 1957*                    *High School of the Air, Brooklyn,*
                                          *New York, USA*

My Dear Mr Holmes,

In our class we have just read 'The Red-Headed League'. Would you please clear up this for us?

1. How did you expect John Clay and his partner to get the gold away? 2. You needed three pipes to think about this case. Why do you smoke so much? 3. You do not mention any interest in athletics. Are you interested in sports? 4. One of our classmates, Bill, bought a combination lock. Only he knows the combination. Last week he opened his locker. Things were missing. Bill claims he locked the lock and used the combination to open it. Can you solve this mystery? Bob thinks we haven't told you enough facts. Bob is also a classmate, with Anthony and Jay who are helping me to write this to you.

We all enjoy your stories. The boys think you are great. May we please have an answer to this so we may read it on the air (radio) to the home-bound students to whom we broadcast our lessons.

Sincerely,
> Lillian Cowen (teacher), Jay, Robert, Anthony, Bill (radio class)


## The Portrait of Hugo Baskerville

*29 August 1957*                                         *Helsinki, Finland*

Dear Mr Holmes!

I just read the book, *The Hound of the Baskervilles* and though it must have happened for a long time ago, I would like to know a thing about it. You must remember the picture of Hugo Baskerville and I want to know who is the artist who has painted it. I hope that you can remember it. Please write me about your results as soon as possible.

Many regards to Dr Watson.

Sincerely yours,
> Esa Helasuvo

*17 October 1957*                                      *London w1*

Dear Mr Helasuvo,

Thank you for your letter of August 29th. Mr Sherlock Holmes is at present absent from London, probably beekeeping in Sussex, and I am therefore answering your letter to the best of my ability.

It is not known for certain who painted the portrait of Hugo Baskerville from which Holmes recognized the kinship of Stapleton to the Baskervilles. It is, however, fairly safe to deduce that, as the family portraits at Baskerville Hall included a Reynolds and a Kneller, it was the tradition of the Baskerville family to be painted by the best-known artists of the time.

There is therefore little doubt that the portrait of Hugo Baskerville, painted in the 1640s while he was serving the cause of Charles I, is the work of Franz Hals, the famous Dutch artist, one of whose best known works is 'The Laughing Cavalier'.

Thank you for your good wishes to Dr Watson. I shall not fail to pass the message on should I see him in the near future.

Yours sincerely,

Donegall, Editor, *Sherlock Holmes Journal*


## Lyn Satterstrom's Letter

*September 1959*                          *Richfield, Minnesota, USA*

Dear Sir,

Although I have been told that you do not really exist, as have the other members of my English class, I still think that somehow you do. In the hearts of all those who read about your wonderful exploits in the world of solving crime, you do exist, as surely as the typewriter on which I write surely does exist – although my typewriting is a far cry from your great feats of crime detection.

I realize you are shy when it comes to a lot of praise, so I will just say that you can never know how proud your readers are of you – that is, all but the detectives who read Dr Watson's stories just to help them solve their own crimes.

Dr Watson said that you are – or were, as the case may be – a rather messy housekeeper. But even your messy stacks of news clippings have helped you to solve crimes, haven't they?

There are suspicious-looking characters around all the time, and some people think you should come to this country to investigate. I have told them repeatedly, of course, that you are much too busy to bother with the crimes of America when you can help your own country.

Well, actually, the reason I wrote is because I want to receive a letter from you so that I will know if you are still living and advancing the detective profession, or if you have passed on the road to happiness. If you are not living, would you kindly let me know? The rest of my English class is anxiously awaiting your letter also.

Did you really do all the things that Dr Watson said you did? Some of the crimes and mysteries you solved seem almost impossible. Well, I must leave you to your work.

In your next spare second or so, would you drop – preferably mail – me a note (by this I mean a letter, of course)? Thank you ever so much.

Sincerely,
Lyn Satterstrom


## The Richfield Request

*September 1959*                                      *Richfield, Minnesota, USA*

My Dear Mr Holmes,

I feel as if I have known you for a very long time, for I have read every one of your adventures as recorded by Dr Watson. I think that you must have a marvellous brain to have escaped alive from some of your cases, let alone solve them. Would you please let me know if there is any fan club of yours around Minneapolis and how to join it. I would really appreciate that. Perhaps you might even include a picture of yourself or your apartment. But if you are too busy with your bees and everything, I will understand.

At the present I am practising some of your techniques. I would really appreciate a pointer here or there, as my imagination always seems to go in the wrong direction. But then you might be reluctant to give out the tricks that make you the world's greatest detective. I have not seen any recent references to your adventures in the newspapers, or was that article about Scotland Yard uncovering a series of murders of wealthy women really your work?

I hope you are in good health.

Very truly yours,
Mary Matos


## Mr Frantzich's Fascination

*8 September 1959*                    *Minneapolis, Minnesota, USA*

Dear Mr Holmes,

I have always been very fascinated by your method of solving crimes. I have read many of the stories which tell about your escapades and I have enjoyed them all very much.

I am very interested in becoming a detective. If possible, could you send me any of your personal suggestions on becoming a detective? Thank you.

Sincerely yours,
Stephen Frantzich

# 'The Art of Detection'

*27 January 1960*                    *Morristown, Pennsylvania, USA*

Dear Mr Holmes,

I have been a fan of yours for about seven years, and I would like to know if you can send me a picture of yourself and your den. I would like to know how you ever got interested in writing books about your work.

If you can send me this information, I would like it as soon as possible.

Sincerely,
            Donald Hughes


# The Kharkov Bet

*24 April 1961*                                *Kharkov, USSR*

Dear Sir,

I make a bet with my friends that I shall receive a letter from Sherlock Holmes himself. Between ourselves, I read in a copy of Polish magazine about such letters and I hope to receive your letter.

Yours truly,
            A. Dunnjevsky

# A Polish Wall Picture

5 February 1962                                    Warsaw, Poland

Dear Sir,

Very you like. I am fourteen year old. I read about you very much. Is
Master best detective in world? A picture your room, please to send.
Does to hang him on the wall.

　With reverence,
　　　　　　　　Pawee Kasprzycki

P.S. Sorry so much error. Learn only two month.

# The Utah Store Theft

6 March 1965                                    Layton, Utah, USA

Dear Mr Holmes,

I have heard and read of your many exploits and admire your
talents. You should be congratulated for your amazing use of scientific
methods in your work.

　I need assistance in a case desperately. You were the best one I
could turn to. Some goods were stolen from my father's store, and,
because of the suspicious nature of the crime, the insurance company
will not pay for the lost goods. We need the money badly and would
appreciate your assistance.

　I will be expecting your answer. Thank you.

　Yours truly,
　　　　　　　　Jerry Billings

# To: Sherlock Holmes,
## 221B Baker Street, Lucens

## *A Biography of the World's First Consulting-Detective*

s w 1

Dear Sir,

I was very interested in the article in the *Telegraph* colour supplement and, as an avid reader of the Sherlock Holmes stories, I would be interested to know more about him.

Although the article made it clear that he never existed as a real person, I was very puzzled to read a book by W. Baring-Gould that gives evidence that Holmes *did* exist. The book, for instance, gives a photograph of Holmes, lists the books he wrote (though I have never

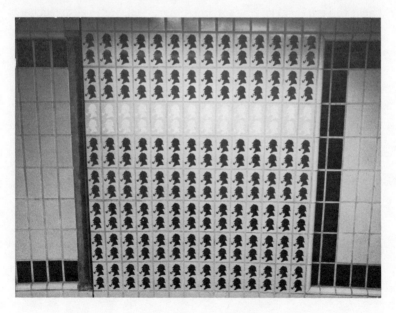

been able to find any of them), tells of meetings between Holmes and Lewis Carroll, Bernard Shaw, etc. Finally it says he died in 1957 aged 103, having just completed his great work, *The Whole Art of Detection*.

I find all this very puzzling, and I wonder whether you could tell me if there was or was not such a person; and, if there was not, then who this book is about, or was it completely invented by the author?

The article mentions that there are various Sherlock Holmes societies. Perhaps you could give me the address of one as I would like to be a member of some such society.

Yours sincerely,
Marian Jarvis

## *The Effingham Affair*

*20 June 1967*                                  *Effingham, Dorking, Surrey*

Dear Sir,

I hear you are very clever at solving things. Well, our English teacher, who is about 84 and looks every day as old as her age, who is very ugly and very strict, is, we think, in fact we are sure, in love with you. We started off by having your book on Monday, but now we have it all week, and she goes round in a dream all the time, swooning, and always has a picture of you.

Love,
Judy LeSeelleur

P.S. Please write back soon – before the end of term – telling us what to do.

P.P.S. Sorry about the speling [*sic*], but we don't do English, we do you instead.

## PART THREE

# Current Correspondence

# [ 1 ]
# Mr Sherlock Holmes

## Sherlock Holmes: Present Whereabouts

*Dayton, Ohio, USA*

Dear Sir,

I should like to inquire the whereabouts of one Sherlock Holmes. I have followed his career quite extensively for some years. Lately though I have not heard much about Mr Holmes. If he is on a bizarre case in some far corner of the world I would like to know. I would also like to know whether he lost his life on one of his very unusual cases.

Yours truly,

David L. Paterson

## A Letter from Mexico

*Puebla Pue, Mexico*

Mr Sherlock Holmes,

I want to congratulate you for your nice job. I admire you as one of the best detectives in the world. In Mexico you have a lot of 'fans'.

I was in England two years ago studying English. I like the climate and the people are so nice.

Well, hope you continue your job.

Your friend,

Augusto Bolonos

# Letter from America

*Springfield, Illinois, USA*

Mr Sherlock Holmes,

Although I have never met you face to face, you appear to be a man of ingenious cleverness; a man with a sharp eye who knows constantly what is happening around him. After reading many of your stories, I find myself more aware of things that happen, and I have even found myself asking a lot of questions lately. Not only this, but I find myself dreaming of being in your position and then awakening during the night in a scared state. Isn't it sort of dangerous in the jobs you do, mostly having no back up for yourself? As I see it, Watson and yourself have private cases which no one except the two of you and your clients know of. Aren't you ever in a position where you are in trouble and there is nobody there to help you?

Oh, don't get me wrong! I feel that your job is appreciated by myself and many more. I just wish that there were more like you doing the same job as you do.

I guess I'll just stick with school for the next five years and maybe go on to college.

Good luck to you!

Sincerely,
> Linda Santini

# The Old Russian Woman

*Moscow, USSR*

Mr Dear Young Friend,

I am an old lady from the Soviet Union and a great admirer of Sherlock Holmes and Baker Street. Mr Conan Doyle is my favourite writer, the writer of my youth. I have read all his stories, novels and articles, in English and in Russian. I have been to London some years ago and visited his Pub but had no time to visit his flat. I'll never forgive myself.

My dear girl, if you have time, please send me some souvenirs (postcards) of Baker Street and of my dearest Sherlock Holmes. I'll send you some Russian books (in English) from Moscow and you will know more about our life. We all love English people, English life, English dogs! I've seen plenty of them in London. I'll never forget my trip there. I think the Spring there is wonderful.

Thank you! I'll wait for your letter and hope to get it. My love to Mr Sherlock Holmes and Mr Watson.

Yours,
    Deanna Chaneles


## The Japanese Image

Saitama, Japan

Dear Mr Holmes,

We love you very much and we have read the complete works of Holmes. We are Japanese girls who are in middle school attached to the Women's University of Japan. We are thinking about what you are like. How splendid and wonderful you are! We have often wondered what Baker Street is like. We would like you to send photographs of your house and Baker Street.

In Japan, there is a song called 'Dr Watson and Mr Sherlock Holmes'. This song does not match the image of you we get from the books. The last time there was a 'Mr Sherlock Holmes adventure' movie on TV we didn't like it. Because it didn't match your image, either.

Some day we will visit you. Please greet Dr Watson for us.

Thank you,
    Akiko Nozawa, Miyoko Harada, Yukari Matui,
    Miki Toita

# A Knight in Indonesia

*Bengkulu, Indonesia*

Sir Sherlock Holmes,

Greeting for you! I hope you don't get frightened when you receive this letter. I'm an admirer of you and I'm very interested in your story. It's very difficult to look for a story book about you. I also like to read the James Bond series (Ian Fleming) and Agatha Christie, but I never meet their address. Then I found your address from magazine of *Tempo* (*Time*).

Now I'm very comfort that I can meet you through this letter. I've one story book about you named *Adventures of Sherlock Holmes* (*Peristawa Aneh dari Sherlock Holmes*) by Sir Arthur Conan Doyle. I can read about the 'Scandal from Bohemia' and I'm very interested with your friend, Mr Watson. Is he still living? Who's Irene Adler? Is this happening true?

Sometimes I'm very surprised about this happening. Is Sir Sherlock Holmes still in living? Could you tell me something about your living and your family? Give me your signature, please, or another thing.

I live in a little town. There are many palm trees and it's a calm town. Now I've worked at Kantor Wilayah Departemen Penerangan Prepinsi Bengkulu (Information Office of Bengkulu Province).

Till this time, we can meet at the next letter. Forgive my mistakes, because I can speak English a little. Remember me to your friend Mr Watson. And so long at the next time.

Sincerely yours,
Zaini Usman

# An Opinion from Poland

*Lublin, Poland*

Dear Sir,

My name is Mariusz Cybulski. I am a Polish boy, sixteen years.

I should like to congratulate you on your magnificent successes. Let me tell my opinion about you, Sir. You are the keenest detective of all time. I am convinced that you work better and faster than all polices, Sir.

My best love to Mr Watson.

Yours faithfully,
Mariusz Cybulski

# From Darkest Africa

*Kumasi Ashanti, Ghana, West Africa*

Dear Sir,

I am with much pleasure to inform you this letter. Before I can say something, I don't know your present condition of health. But I think by the Grace of God you are fine in Abbey House. Please, I am a boy of thirteen years, but I want to take you as my penpal, but I don't know you. Please, I beg you to send me some of your money or anything you like to send.

Please, if you will understand to take me as your friend, then please add your picture and send it to me which can show me that you will understand. I end here with much greetings to you. May God bless you all the time, Amen. Goodbye now.

Yours faithfully,
Kwame Frempong

# The Girl from Oxon Hill

*Oxon Hill, Maryland, USA*

Dear Mr Holmes,

You sure are a good detective! I know a man who is a detective in my town. He doesn't do all the neat stuff you do and he dresses in regular, everyday clothes. He's nice though.

I read all of your books. I get one (or two) out every time we go the public library.

My mom says you're not really a person but that Mr Doyle made you up. I told her that Mr Doyle is your friend and he writes your books 'cuz you're too busy.

Say 'hi' to Dr Watson for me.

Sincerely,
 Lyn Smith


# The Contented Heart

*Setagaya-ku, Tokyo, Japan*

Dear Mr Sherlock Holmes,

Hello, I'm a Japanese girl. My name is Junko Nakane. I am your fan. I like you. I want to have your room picture because I have never been to Baker Street. I read a lot of your books.

I like you from the bottom of my heart. I want to speak to my heart's content with you. I enjoyed your story to my heart's content. Thank you, Mr Sherlock Holmes!

Goodbye,
 Junko Nakane

# Mohamed Salim of India

*Trivandrum, Kerala, India*

Dear Sherlock Holmes,

I am much honoured by writing a letter to you because you are the world's greatest genius of a detective I have ever seen. Oh, what a fantastic escape you had from that worst waterfall! Dear genius, the most unfortunate thing at present is I am reading your *Return of Sherlock Holmes* and that is the only book I have received in my life after taking much trouble. Oh God, how I waited and waited for a single book of yours. But the happiest moment of my life is yet to come. That is my friend offered to give me every series of your book. Thanks to God, thanks to Conan Doyle and thanks very much to you for the world's most beautiful adventures.

I heard that your people are sending catalogues to those who write you letters. I also want the same. Not only that, I want your reply also. Won't you honour me with a reply?

Now I reveal my identity. My name is Mohamed Salim H. A. of age twenty-seven, still a B.A. student doing business. My hobbies are book reading (especially yours) and seeing English movies. I would very much like to visit your country, alas my circumstances are not right. But one day I will visit you and your country. Moreover how could we Indians forget the British, at least they were here for a hundred years of ruling. I am very sad and sorry to take leave from this dramatic scene. I wish to God that you would honour me with an early reply. Hope you are in the best of health. Wishing you all the best. Long live the genius Sherlock Holmes!

Your greatest fan,
Mohamed Salim H.A.

THIS PLAQUE
COMMEMORATES THE
HISTORIC MEETING EARLY
IN 1881 AT THE ORIGINAL
CRITERION LONG BAR
OF D<sup>R</sup> STAMFORD AND
D<sup>R</sup> JOHN H. WATSON
WHICH LED TO THE INTRODUCTION
OF D<sup>R</sup> WATSON TO
M<sup>R</sup> SHERLOCK HOLMES

HERE, NEW YEARS DAY, 1881
AT THE CRITERION LONG BAR
STAMFORD, DRESSER AT BARTS

MET

## DR. JOHN H. WATSON

AND LED HIM TO IMMORTALITY

AND

## SHERLOCK HOLMES

The Sherlock Holmes Society of London
and The Baker Street Irregulars · 1981
by The Inverness Capers of Akron, Ohio

# The Sakai Ability Screed

*Taki-gun, Hyogo-ken, Japan*

My Dear Mr Holmes,

How do you do? I am your fan in Japan. I'm sorry that I am not good at English.

I like detective stories very much. So I have read a lot of story of you. I am sure that you are more wonderful than any other private detective. Not only I, but also my friend says so. Why are you so ability? I want to become like you. If so, I would have been in favour. Don't think that is a matter of no importance.

Then I wish you will be active. Please remember me to your assistant (I know his name, but I don't know its spelling. I'm sorry).

Very truly yours,
Yukari Sakai

# Donna Dunn's Paper

*Takoma Park, Maryland, USA*

Dear Mr Holmes,

I have an incredible problem on my hands and I would greatly appreciate your help in solving it. You see, within the past month I have found myself struggling along with a quite difficult term paper in English. What may surprise you is that I finally decided to undertake a paper concerning yourself. Finding myself in need of references, I decided to turn to the person who knows you best of all. If you could be of any assistance to me by sending some information, I would be most grateful. Take care and give my regards to Watson.

Sincerely,
Donna M. Dunn

# The York History Student

*University of York, York*

Dear Mr Holmes,

I hope you do not mind me writing to you – I realize that you are a very busy man and that you do not greatly care, at the best of times, for the praise you so deserve. However, I felt it my duty to write and thank you. I am a university student, studying history, and where I can, I apply your methods. The end result of this is that I find I am able to ask questions no one else has thought of. Thanks to you, my essays receive high marks and are individual. I believe Dr Watson's accounts of your exploits should be compulsory reading at university – they are that helpful.

Once again, from the bottom of my heart, God bless you, Mr Holmes!

Yours faithfully,

Stephen Phillips


## The German Abitur

*Russelsheim a. Main, West Germany*

Dear Sir,

I am writing to you because I am a great fan of Sherlock Holmes and I want to write my Abitur (German 'A' level) work on him. I have ready many of his books and am very interested in him.

I would be very happy if you could send me some books or pamphlets with information about Sherlock Holmes to help me for my research and exams. Thanking you in advance, I eagerly await your reply.

Yours sincerely,

Markus Sauer

# The Missouri Scholar

Dear Mr Holmes,

As a scholar at the University of Missouri I am quite aware of your position and of the respect in which you are held. Your memoirs and casebooks inscribed by Dr Watson have for many years left me breathless with excitement. I am also a keen fan of the movie series shown on television twice a week here in Missouri. These give a visual account of some of your more brilliant cases. Ah! to know more. I have searched the records and books in the University Library to no avail. They have only one shelf of books. I would be ever so grateful to know more about your exciting life and also to have a list of publications and memorabilia which are on sale in the United Kingdom. I fully intend to visit 221B Baker Street as soon as I am out of school and financially secure. Until then, please accept a hearty 'bravo' from an admirer of long standing. You are truly a magnificent personality.

Cordially yours,
Gregg Eliot Robbins

# From a Correspondent
# in Ujung-Pandang

*Ujung-Pandang, Indonesia*

Dear Sir,

What a surprise it was when a person told me that you still live in London at present. I would like to know more about you, although I have learnt much from Mr Conan Doyle.

Wish you all the best of happiness.

Yours truly,
Hasnah Ibrahim

55

## The Undying Detective

*Örebro, Sweden*

Dear Sir, Sherlock Holmes,

I don't know much about you och that is why I write and ask: How do you live? or are you dead? I am happy if I get some information about that!

Yours sincerely,
Maya-Lüra Romppainen

## The Baker Street Interloper

*Gaitersburg, Maryland, USA*

Dear Mr Sherlock Holmes,

I like your stories very much. In one book it said you were dead. Were you ever alive? Or was someone using your name and made up the stories? Are the stories all true? Would you please write back and send a list of all of your books.

Thank you very much,
Pam Wright

## Beyond the Grave

*Avondale, Georgia, USA*

Dear Mr Sherlock Holmes,

My teacher told me that you aren't real. I hope she is lying because I watched all of your movies and spent lots of money on your books. I would be very disappointed if this is true. Please write back and let me know – even if you have to send it by *grave mail*!

Thank you,
　　　　Belinda Sauthreaux


## *Sherlockian Faction*


*Farmington, Michigan, USA*
Mr Sherlock Holmes,

I have read some of the books about you and I have become very interested in the way you work. Some of your cases are really fantastic. I will get right to the point: I have a bet with a friend who says you never lived. I say you do. Will you please send me an autographed picture of you so I can prove you are alive. Thank you.

Sincerely yours,
　　　　Larry Collins

# The Counterfeit Claim

*Springfield, Illinois, USA*

Dear Sherlock,

How can you stand all of those scary mysteries? One kid in my class said that you are a phoney! How old are you? Do you have any kids? If so, how many? Have you and Dr Watson solved any more mysteries? Well, bye!

Your friend,
Lisa Suter


# A Sham Sherlock Holmes

*Muskegon, Missouri, USA*

Dear Mr Holmes,

I would appreciate it if you would answer this question for me, one which I hardly like to ask. Are you a fake? I have heard stories of this sort which suggest that you are. As for myself, I do not believe these rumours.

I hope that you will be able to answer this question.

Sincerely yours,
Karen Boersema


# The Existence of Him

*Osaka, Japan*

Dear Sherlock Holmes,

I am your fan. I have a brother. He is your fan, too. We were reading some of your stories. I think you a wonderful detective. I believe the existence of you.

Please give me a letter.

Katsuhiko Imamura

# The Time of Full Activity

*Itabashi-ku, Tokyo, Japan*

Dear Mr Sherlock Holmes,

You might probably be very surprised to receive this letter from a stranger. For a long time I have wanted to write a letter to you. I praise you for your activity.

Allow me to introduce myself. I am a girl of sixteen in my second year of senior high school. I was born and brought up in Tokyo. I like mystery novels very much. I am a great fan of yours.

Your time of full activity is not passed. You have eternal life and you are loved by the world's people.

Give my wishes to Mr Watson.

Very sincerely yours,

Yayoi Ito


# The Second Mr Holmes

*Springfield, Ohio, USA*

Dear Mr Holmes,

I would like to know if you're the real Sherlock Holmes who was made up in the eighteen hundreds? Or were you the second to live? You know, like Lassie and Tarzan? And what made you become a detective in the movie? Did you go to law school and were you ever in the Force? When you were solving the Jack the Ripper case, were you scared? How long has it been since you have made a movie?

Sincerely yours,

Chris Steele

## Sholto's Problem

*Herne Hill, London* SE 24

Dear Sherlock Holmes,

I was having an argument with my friend about whether or not you are real. I said you were real, and my friend said you do not exist. So I went up to the teacher and asked her, and she said you don't exist. But still I read your books and I think they're great. The one I got today is *The Hound of the Baskervilles*. I also watch you on the tele.

Yours sincerely,
Sholto Haggart

## La Vida es Sueno

*Ha Tiogi City, Tokyo, Japan*

Dear Sherlock Holmes,

I'm sorry that you are living at everyone's dream.

I read *A Study in Scarlet*, *The Sign of Four*, *The Hound of the Baskervilles*, *The Return of Sherlock Holmes*, *The Valley of Fear*, and *The Casebook of Sherlock Holmes*. I like best the *Study* and the *Hound*.

Take care of your health. Good night.

Let's meet at dream,
Shintani Isao

# The Living Dead

*Winnipeg, Manitoba, Canada*

Dear Mr Holmes,

Why would a logical and reasonable teenager write to an obviously long-dead person such as you? The answer is that in my mind, as well as in the minds of countless others the world over, you shall remain the most immortal man in history, whether in fiction or non-fiction.

I write in the hope that you will send to me a copy of your autograph.

Yours sincerely,

Wayne Preston

## The Secret of Eternal Life

*Windsor, Ontario, Canada*

Dear Mr Holmes,

For some time now, I have been reading about your detective cases, so well recorded by your good friend, Dr Watson. I have often wondered how you have managed to live up to this date considering you were born in 1854. I have heard that you eat Royal Jelly to prolong life. Is this true?

Is your home still in Baker Street? Do you still do detective work? I have always admired you as a person and believe you exist, despite the rumours to the contrary. I will always think of you as the greatest detective of all time and will cherish any answer from you.

Yours sincerely,

David Devereux

# The Real Sherlock Holmes

*Willowdale, Ontario, Canada*

My Dear Mr Holmes,

Greetings from Canada! I have been a great admirer of yours for several years. I must say that I am amazed at your remarkable longevity. I am writing to wish you best wishes on your recent birthday. May you have many more.

I am constantly astounded to find references to the 'fictional' detective Sherlock Holmes. I find that I am constantly coming to your defence and have had some run-ins with the local library authorities after I removed the stories of your adventures off of the fiction shelves and placed them in 'biographies' where they rightly belong.

Please accept my apologies for the belatedness of the birthday wishes, and believe me to be,

Faithfully yours,

Bob Coghill

# The Biographical Quest

*Cuyahoga Falls, Ohio, USA*

Dear Mr Holmes,

Recently I read of a case called 'The Speckled Band'. I must commend you on your brilliant deductions in solving it.

I, myself, am interested in mysteries and, you being my favourite detective, I was prompted to write to you. My colleague and I are interested in some information pertaining to your biography. I would be overwhelmed at the thought of receiving some data on your encounters.

I will be anxiously awaiting your reply.

Sincerely yours,

Dave Rodriguez

# Indian Blood

*Ottawa, Ontario, Canada*

Dear Sir,

What do you say about statements that were made in the Bootmakers' Club in Toronto, Ontario, that you are part Indian and grew up near Winnipeg, Manitoba?

Apparently that club came to the conclusion that there are clues in *A Study in Scarlet* to indicate that your black sheep grandfather might have been disowned and sent to the Red River settlement on the Prairies.

The Indian blood is apparently suggested in your hawk-like appearance and your genius at tracking.

The Bootmakers' Club got its name from a passing reference to a bootmaker from Toronto in *The Hound of the Baskervilles*.

The latest from this club is that Dr Watson was a vaguely shady character who lived and practised on Avenue Road in Toronto for twenty-nine years. Toronto lawyer Hartley Nathan explained that he was checking a property title when he learned that the previous owner was a Dr John Henry Watson.

Is any of this true?

Sincerely,

Margaret Kerr

# The Parents of Sherlock Holmes

*Bollnas, Sweden*

Dear Mr Holmes,

I want you to answer a few questions about your childhood. Where were you born? What are your parents' names? And to what school did you go?

I would be very thankful for an answer to these questions.

Yours faithfully,

Bjorn Jonsson

# Mr Holmes, Senior

*Springfield, Illinois, USA*

Mr Sherlock Holmes,

I would like to ask you some questions. Where were you born and how did you come to be a detective? Was your father a detective? Also, in 'The Empty House', how did you know that Watson would still be in London?

When you reply, please enclose a picture of yourself. I want your picture to prove that you really are alive and not a fake.

Your fan,
> Steve


# The Boyhood of Sherlock Holmes

*Dynas, Sweden*

Dear Mr Holmes,

I have always wondered how old you were when you solved a crime for the first time. What kind of crime was it? I mean, was it a bank robbery, did you capture a burglar, or was it something else?

Did you read detective novels when you were a little boy? What case was the most difficult to solve, and how did you solve it? I have always thought that you never use weapons. Is it true, or have you ever used a gun or some other weapon?

Well, I will close now because I know you are a very busy man, but I would be most grateful if you had time to answer these questions.

Kindest regards from one of your admirers,
> Christer Nilsson

P.S. You must not forget to give my best regards to Dr Watson.

# Schooldays

*Axvall, Sweden*

To Mr Sherlock Holmes's Private Secretary,

Hello! I've just read about Mr Holmes and his immortal reputation. I know he has not got enough time to answer the letters in person, so I hope you can answer some questions about him.

I think I've read all the books about him, but I don't remember if there is something about his schools in one of them. I mean, in which kind of schools has he gone? And can he speak many languages?

Perhaps Mr Holmes has got a little time to spare so he can solve this problem? Looking forward to your answer.

With best regards,
Pertti Koivuaho

# The Early Career of Sherlock Holmes

*Garden City, New York, USA*

Dear Mr Holmes,

I would like a rough idea of your background. Where did you find Watson? Where did you first use the words 'Elementary School'? What was the first case you cracked wide open? How old were you when you started being a detective? Is it true that you were at first a doctor and didn't like it, so you got interested in detective work? And where did you go to school?

I especially liked *The Hound of the Baskervilles*. It was extremely interesting. I also like the way you talk. What kind of accent do you talk with?

Sincerely,
Robby Shields

# Marriage Plans

*Fresno, California, USA*

Dear Mr Holmes,

I am a great admirer of yours. I have a few questions to ask you and hopefully you will answer them. Have you ever married, or have you any plans to marry? Have you seen anything of your brother lately? What is he doing? Do you have any other living relatives? Can you tell me where I can locate Dr Watson? And is Professor Moriarty still up to his old tricks?

Very truly yours,
Stephanie Agar

# Children*

Dear Dr Holmes,

I would like you to send me pictures of some famous places in London.
Did you really have two children? One named Jacky and the other a baby?
Well, better be going now. Write back soon.

Sincerely,
Tami Cooper

---

* A misreading of 'The Sussex Vampire'

## Mrs Sherlock Holmes

*Deer Park, New York, USA*

Dear Sir,

I am a very big fan of yours. I would like to know why in all of your stories no one ever mentions your wife. Are you married? If so, what is her name? I would also like to know how old you are.

Sincerely yours,
Louis Riccatti


## Arsène Lupin

*Tokyo, Japan*

Dear Mr Sherlock Holmes,

I'm pleased that I can write to you. I don't know so much about you, but I like you and your friend Mr Watson. And also, I like your enemy, that is your friend, Arsène Lupin.

About me: I'm a girl. I'm thirteen years old. I'm Japanese. I like to read mystery stories. I like Sherlock Holmes. I like Arsène Lupin. I like a boy that is nice, pleasant and clever.

Some questions: Do you have a wife? Do you like Arsène Lupin? Why did you become a secret agent?

When there is a queer incident in Japan, would you come here? Oh! How I want your reasoning powers! When I was in Juniors, I wanted to be a detective. I still want to know more about the activities that you've done.

Best wishes to you and to your friend, Mr Watson.

From a Japanese girl that likes you,
Kumiko M

## Herlock Sholmès

*Evian, France*

Herlock Sholmès,

I hope you are of health. I'm reading all your books. You are the most intelligent man in the world. I will want to go to England. I believe I'm going soon with my school. I hope that we can visit your house.

Goodbye,
    Cachat Bertrand

## A Norwegian Explorer

*Alvundeid, Norway*

Dear Mr Sherlock Holmes,

We in Norway would like to have some informations about Mr Sherlock Holmes. Where is he buried? How old was he?

Would you please send some informations about him. Maybe you have a little book or something you can send us.

We are just now reading a book about him, it is 'The Speckled Band'.

Your faithful,
    Asbjørn Valset

# The Heirs of Sherlock Holmes

*Dept of Religion, Sir George Williams University,*
*Montreal, Canada*

Sirs,

I am interested in locating the heirs, if any, of the late Sherlock Holmes, the private investigator. Any information which you might provide would be most welcome.

With many thanks for your kind co-operation, I remain,

Sincerely,
Jonathan P. Siegel

# The Odessa Plaque Proposal

*Leninsk, Andizhan Region, USSR*

Dear Madam,

I have read an article the other day in our daily *Komsomolskay Pravda*. The correspondent wrote that you are in charge of the late Cherlock Holmes's affairs.

In the same article a certain map is mentioned that is displayed in the Cherlock Holmes bar in Trafalgar Square. What interests me is the fact that Odessa – our Black Sea port – is marked on that map, as a place that once had been visited by Mr Holmes.

As I am planning to go to that city myself during these summer vacations, I would greatly appreciate your looking through the late Mr Holmes's papers with the purpose of finding out: When was he in that city? Where did he stay there? If Mr Holmes took a lodging in an hotel, then what hotel? If he stayed in a boarding-house, what was the street and the house number?

If you think that you could manage to furnish me with such information, I believe that some sort of a memorial plate could be inaugurated there, as a modest token of tribute to your world-famous compatriot.

Hoping to hear from you soon.

Most sincerely yours,
Joseph Shelestian

## The Japanese New Year Greetings Card

*Yokosuka City, Kanagawa Prefecture, Japan*

A Happy New Year, Mr Sherlock Holmes!

The card is used only for congratulations on New Year's day in Japan. I'm a Japanese University student. I first read of your activity ten years ago. I think, 'What a wonderful and emotional story this is!' Since then I read all your stories which have been put on sale in Japan. I want you to be active in Japan. Then I won't read other detective stories. Besides, if I have the chance, I'll go to England and visit your house. So, I must study English. I'm sorry that the sentence be poor and mistaken. But I'm going to read your story that I can find and are sold in Japan.

Be careful to catch a cold! And please remember Mr Watson. If possible, may I have a letter?

So long,
Wataru Ohkawa

## Birthday Wishes

*Woodlands Hills, California, USA*

Dear Mr Holmes,

I would like to personally wish you a happy birthday, even though you may get this letter a day or two late. I found out your birthday from our English teacher, whom I believe you have had the pleasure of meeting.

71

She has told us many interesting things about you and your good friend, Dr H. Watson. Although many of my classmates have some doubts about you and Dr Watson being real people, I have no doubts at all. I am having a hard time convincing others of your reality, so could you please send me some kind of proof that would help me at my task. Thank you so very much.

Your admirer,
Dave Cooperman

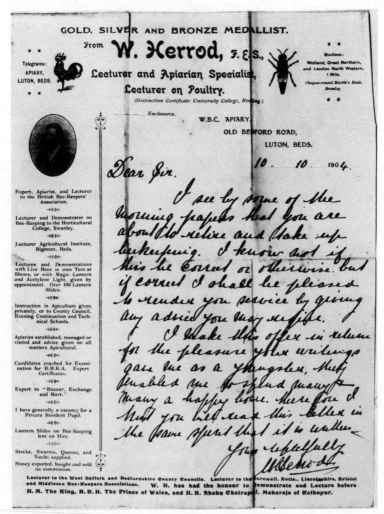

# A LETTER OF SALUTATION AND FELICITATION PRESENTED TO MR SHERLOCK HOLMES ON THE OCCASION OF HIS ONE HUNDRED AND TWENTIETH BIRTHDAY

MAY YOUR BIRTHDAY BE BLESSED WITH PEACE AND JOY AND HAPPINESS AND MAY GOD'S CHOICEST BLESSINGS BE YOURS THIS COMING YEAR

*Oak Park, Delaware, USA*

Mr Holmes,

I have admired your prowess as a consulting detective for over nine years and only just now did I even think of sending you a card to inform you of the fact. Happy 120th Birthday!

With admiration,
David Corbett

## The Compliments of the Season

*Musashino City, Tokyo, Japan*

TO MR SHERLOCK HOLMES AND DR WATSON

MERRY CHRISTMAS AND A HAPPY NEW YEAR!

FROM MARI IWAI

## Mr Holmes Rising

*Hikawa-gun, Semane, Japan*

Dear Mr Holmes,

What time do you get up? What time do you go to bed? Is it very cold in the morning? Please write soon.

Sincerely yours,
Masato Hurakawa


## Clutter

*Portland, Oregon, USA*

Dear Sir,

After hearing Dr Watson's reminiscences of your most famous cases over the BBC, I felt I should write to you. Congratulations on solving these cases!

One way we are alike is that although our rooms seem to be a mess, we can find whatever we want in the clutter.

I wish you continued success in your crime-solving. I would like to hear from you; and, if possible, would you please use commemorative stamps for postage?

Sincerely yours,
David Brock

P.S. Have a very Merry Christmas!

## The Baker Street Bathrooms

*Roslyn, Long Island, USA*

Dear Sir,

About Sherlock Holmes, one bathroom or two?

Claude Solnik

## The Telegraph and the Telephone

*Ekeroe, Sweden*

Dear Sir,

I have recently read (of course, not for the first time) some of your cases, presented by Mr Conan Doyle (who, I presume, is a pseudonym for Dr Watson). As a result, I would like to ask a few questions.

Is Mr Doyle the same person as Dr Watson? In that case, I think your friend is an excellent writer.

To solve some of your cases I have noticed that you have to take decisions and make certain contacts very rapidly. Acting as you do, you are often very successful. But I have often wondered why do you always use the telegraph? From my own experience I have found that the telephone is an instrument with many advantages. I'm sure you must have a telephone and, since you are a man of great intelligence and experience, there is certainly an explanation. Could you please tell me why you think that the telegraph is superior? Or could you think about trying the telephone? In these days I have heard there is a lot of illegal listening to other people's telephone calls. Could this be the reason?

Dear Mr Holmes, would you be so kind to lighten my mind and tell me. I hope to be able to go to London some day and – at least – take a look at your famous house in Baker Street.

Yours sincerely,

Robert Engstroem

# General Inquiries

*Foley, Minnesota, USA*

Dear Mr Holmes,

We would like to know some things about you. What are your fees, what are your hobbies (besides being a detective), and what foods do you like? Also, do you have a pipe and hat like they show in the movies?

We would like to know this and to receive any other information you can give us about your work and your life. Thank you.

Sincerely,

Mary Walters, Patty Paggen


# Further Questions

*Spartanburg, South Carolina, USA*

Dear Mr Holmes,

I have read one of your novels, *The Hound of the Baskervilles*, as well as a play presentation of 'The Case of the Beryl Coronet'. Needless to say, your sheer logic astounded me. I trust that you will not fail to detect my sincerity in hoping that you will reply to the following questions.

How do you feel when you have solved a case? Also, what factors determine whether or not you will take a case? How and when did you begin the art of detection? How do you go about solving a mystery?

Eagerly awaiting your reply, I remain,

Yours truly,

Trip Payne

## How it Feels to be a Detective

*Cave Junction, Oregon, USA*

Dear Mr Holmes,

In one of my classes we read a play about you. I have never read a book about you before, but I really enjoyed this play very much.

Well, my teacher told us that one of his classes last year had written to you and that you had answered them back.

Sir, I would be very grateful if you would please write a letter back to me. I would just like a little information on how it feels to be a very well-known detective.

Thank you,
Shellie Mason

## The Most Interesting Adventure

*Warsaw, Poland*

Dear Mr Sherlock Holmes,

Your mysterious cases are very interesting for me and I like books of your adventures very much. I would like to get some information about your most interesting adventure, i.e. the one you like best. Please, write to me about it.

Kindest regards to you and Dr Watson.

Yours sincerely,
Maciej Janowski

## The Hardest Case

*Kingsbury Mission Hills, California, USA*
Dear Mr Sherlock Holmes,

I have heard about some of the cases you have solved. I am very interested in your ability to solve hard cases. What was the hardest of all? How long did it take you to solve it? Maybe if you have another case you might want to send a letter explaining it to me and I might help you solve it.

Your friend,
Mark Pogue

## First Meeting with Dr Watson

*Vienna, Austria*
Dear Mr Holmes,

I am an Austrian girl and I like to read your stories. I am a curious girl and have some questions. Why are you so clever and solve all secrets? From where do you know Dr Watson? So you like to be a detective?

Maybe you can write me something about you. Best wishes to Dr Watson!

Your
Martina Heibl

## Dr Watson Again, and an Unethical Question

*Deer Park, New York, USA*

Dear Mr Holmes,

I often wondered how you met Dr Watson and what was your hardest mystery and have you ever made love to any of your clients?

Sincerely yours,
Robert Lawrence


## Some Observations Upon Mr Sherlock Holmes

[With particular reference to the current problems of the United States of America]

*Charleston, West Virginia, USA*

Dear Mr Holmes,

I've been reading *The Hound of the Baskervilles*, and I thought I might write to you and tell you what I think of it. I thought you did a very good job on figuring out the mystery, but, of course, you always do that. When I first started reading it I thought it was boring but by the time I got to the end I liked it.

I would also like your opinion on whether you think the United States is ever going to get straightened out.

Hope I didn't take too much of your time!

Sincerely,
Lisa Fridley

## Crime in New York

*New York, USA*

Dear Sir,

I understand you are a great detective. I would like to know how you would go about dealing with the increasing rate of crime in New York. Please send me some of your suggestions on how I should prevent myself from being a victim of crime.

Sincerely yours,
Patrick Devlin

## Legal Contrasts

*Lubbock, Texas, USA*

Dear Mr Holmes,

I would be interested in knowing the basic differences between the law enforcement procedures of England and those of America. I do not expect a lengthy report but rather a brief statement. Thank you for your consideration in this matter.

Sincerely yours,
Randy Armstrong

## Sherlock Holmes – His Limits

*Espeland, Norway*

Dear Mr Sherlock Holmes,

I have just read the book, *A Study in Scarlet*, and wonder if I could ask you a few questions. In one of your first talks with Dr Watson, you declared that you didn't know anything about our Solar System. Many people did not, because they took more interest in what was going on on the earth. Nothing to say about that, but I do not agree when you say that the brain can only absorb matters up to a defined limit. I know you said that many years ago, so with your position to science I am sure that you today would agree when the scientists declare that the human brain is so fantastic that its absorbing of knowledge is without any limit. So you can put into the brain whatever you want: 'Science, Poetry, Music, Sport-results, and so on, Question and Answer!' The brain will keep it without being overcrowded.

My next observation concerns Dr Watson's remark as to your interest in good literature: 'Nil.'

I'm a simple man, Mr Holmes, so I hope you will excuse me for boring you in your busy employment. I hope you will understand my English – I have no chance to practise the language in my daily work, but I've tried to do my best in writing the letter. And then I hope you will take time to answer my questions:

1. Do you agree that the development has shown that your opinion of the human brain was wrong?

2. Even if you can borrow good books at the public library, in my opinion a home without books is a 'poor' home. So much more as in our straining time a good book will give you the relaxing you so absolutely need. Can you say anything about that too?

I follow your further adventures with interest. My love to England, Dr Watson and yourself.

From yours,
        Johannes Eriksen


## The Travelling Coat, Cap and Lens

*Lakeside, California, USA*

Dear Sherlock Holmes and Dr Watson,

You are the best detective on earth and I have read about a hundred of your books. Will you please get me a hat, a cape and a magnifying-glass just exactly like yours.

Sincerely,
        Bob Werner

## A Letter from Seneca

*West Seneca, New York, USA*

Dear Mr Holmes,

We have read a lot of your stories and are going to see a couple of your movies. I love the way you can figure out some of these crimes. You and Colombo are my favourite detectives.

Your coat and hat are really *cool*! And your pipe is super *tough*!

I will always be your fan.

Andy di Giambattista

## The Deerstalker

*Hickory, North Carolina, USA*

Dear Sherlock Holmes,

I have always wanted a hat like you wear and I can't find one in my home town anywhere.

Do you know where I could get one?

Thank you,

David Weaver

## Violins and Virtuosity

*Long Island, New York, USA*

Dear Sir,

I play the violin, and I would like to know the name of Holmes's violin composition. And is it true that his favourite composer is Paganini?

Could you please send me evidence that proves Sherlock Holmes is still living? I have many friends who, far from realizing that he is immortal, doubt his very existence! Their ignorance sometimes hurts. I know that a recent picture is impossible as he keeps so much to himself, but maybe you could get his autograph or something for me.

My gratitude always,
> Claire Brennan


## The Stradivarius

*Edsbyn, Sweden*

Dear Mr Holmes,

I have read a lot of your stories and I admire you very much.

I have noticed that you are a keen violin player and because of that, I would like to ask you what kind of violin you have, how much it is worth and if it is for sale?

Yours faithfully,
> Hokan Jonsall


## A Polyphonic Motet

*Long Island, New York, USA*

Dear Mr Holmes,

In your movies, plays and books it is frequently mentioned that one of your favourite pastimes is playing the violin. What is your favourite piece, classical or otherwise?

Thank you,
> J. Victoria Shaw

## Bradley's Fine Baker Street Blends

*Tlell, British Columbia, Canada*

Dear Mr Holmes,

My husband and I have been avid fans and followers for many years.

My husband is a consistent pipe smoker. He has tried many brands of tobacco throughout the years, but as yet he has had no success in finding a brand that really pleases him. We would like to know what brand you smoke – or if it is a special blend. Do you think we could be so bold as to ask for a sample of your tobacco? The reason we are asking for yours, sir, is that you never seem to be without a pipe. We are sure that your tobacco must be truly fine.

We will feel greatly honoured to receive a reply from such a famous person as yourself.

Thank you,
>           L. Waring


## On Various Distinctive Tobaccos

*Coulsdon, Surrey*

Dear Mr Sherlock Holmes,

When I read your stories as set down by John Watson, M.D., I can't help wondering what tobacco you both smoke, and the cost of it at the turn of the century. I would be most grateful if you could enlighten me.

Yours very sincerely,
>           Nikolas Lawrence

# The Arcadia Mixture

*Winchester, Massachusetts, USA*

Dear Mr Holmes,

I have read some of your short, but exciting adventures in *The Memoirs of Sherlock Holmes*. I would like to congratulate you for your knowledge of things around you and your fine skill at fitting clues together to solve the cases. I also give congratulations to Dr Watson for his writing talent.

If possible, I would like to know more things concerning you and your cases. It may become a hobby for me. If you could just send me a picture of your Baker Street home and some of Dr Watson's Arcadia mixture of tobacco from his bachelor days, I would be contented.

I have almost arrived at the closing of this letter, so I just wanted you to know I think you're the best uncomplicated detective in London.

Sincerely,
> Christopher Arnott

# The Contents of the Persian Slipper

*Hamburg, West Germany*

Dear Mr Holmes,

Please, would you answer me two questions? The first one is: What sort of tobacco are you smoking in your pipe? The second: How old are you now and how long do you know Watson?

I hope you would answer me my questions and so I wish you good luck for your further work.

Yours truly,
> André Hesselbart

## The Cocaine Question

*Buffalo Grove, Illinois, USA*

Dear Mr Holmes,

Could you please tell me why you got hooked on cocaine? How did
your assistant, Dr Watson, go about getting you off the drug? How
long did it take him to get you off the drug?

Sincerely yours,
Dominick Tufano

## Narcotics and Men of Mark

*Farnborough, Hampshire*

Dear Sir,

I heard about you on the radio or television and that you answered
all the letters addressed to Sherlock Holmes.

Was it usual for men of Holmes's stature to take narcotics, especially
in the form of cocaine injections, or was it just considered a minor sin
as smoking?

Yours sincerely,
Eleanor Jowitt

## Underworld Rumours

*Cambridge, Massachusetts, USA*

Dear Sir,

Recently I have come across some rather persistent rumours which
connect you with the drug culture, and espionage in collaboration

with a foreign female spy. Although I do not believe the rumours, I find it hard to convince those who believe it. I hope that in the near future you will make a public statement concerning these rumours. I hate to see the reputation of a good man tarnished by lies.

Sincerely,
Larry L. Lyon

## The Drug-Eater and his Books

*Lawrence, Indiana, USA*

Dear Sherlock Holmes,

We just finished reading one of your mysteries, 'The Case of the Sussex Vampire'. We would like to know if you turned out to be a junky; and, if so, why? We would also like to know how your reputation got started, what was your Number One best-seller and how much money did you make from it?

Thank you for your co-operation.

Sincerely yours,
Laura Robinette, Karen White, Mike Peipu,
Allen Sizemore, Randy Padgett, Joe Nevitt

## The Prague Textbook

*Prague, Czechoslovakia*

Dear Mr Holmes,

Every time, while reading the Adventures of yours and other cases, I have been very much excited by the marvellous ability of your clear, precise and prompt thinking, resulting in a brief, bright and proper analysis of immensely complicated situations. That is why I envy you a little. However, that is because of what I admire you for mostly.

On occasion of reading *The Valley of Fear*, I have got the idea to use some of your phrases as a motto to some chapters of my textbook on Structured Programming I am just now writing.

I should like to ask your kindness to give me permission to reprint some of the translated sentences and sayings of yours in my textbook.

Sincerely yours,
Anthony Carda

P.S. Be so kind, please, as to give my kindest regards to your friend and fellow, Dr Watson.


## The Monograph on Tobacco Ash

*Baldwin, New York, USA*

Dear Mr Holmes,

I would appreciate your sending me a copy of the monograph on cigar and cigarette ashes that you compiled and which has apparently helped you solve many mysteries.

If there is any charge I will be happy to send a cheque by return air mail. Thank you.

Sincerely,
Helen E. Heinrich

## On Secret Writings

*New Kensington, Pennsylvania, USA*

Dear Sherlock Holmes,

I am writing to you because I have been collecting codes and ciphers.
I read about you and your famous cipher mystery, 'The Adventure of
the Dancing Men'. I also seem to recall that you said: 'I, myself, have
solved over one hundred and fifty codes and ciphers.' Therefore, I am
asking you, do you have time to send me some good codes? And, if
possible, a few books about them. If you are busy on another famous
unsolved case, tell me about it.

Yours faithfully,
Al Mauroni

# A Detective's Notebooks

*Machida-City, Tokyo, Japan*

Dear Mr Sherlock Holmes,

Why don't you compose a new note? Is that because of no particular affair? I regret that I have not read a new one since then. But it is very good that the world doesn't give you trouble.

By the way, I am a middle-aged man. I live in a city far from Tokyo which is the capital of Japan. I finished pretty to read your note translated into Japanese. So, now, I have read one in the original little by little.

Looking forward to having your letter.

Your eternal reader,

J. Kihara


# Sherlock Holmes –
# Author

*North Hollywood, California, USA*

My Dear Sherlock Holmes,

With regard to the successful conclusions to the majority of the cases presented to you as a last resort, I would like to congratulate you and wish you continued success.

I have been a faithful follower of yours since I acquired the skill to read. Someday I wish to be able to carry on in your great tradition and solve intriguing mysteries and cases.

At present I have no case in which I would like your great guidance, though if in the future I run across such a case, I will contact you.

When you again return to the USA, as you did in the movie, *Sherlock Holmes goes to Washington*, please contact me, and we can discuss some of your cases as this would help me with my future career.

Your singular methods of crime fighting are very beautifully described by your comrade, Dr Watson. I would like to offer my congratulations to him, as well. Though you, too, are very descriptive when you relate a story, such as the case of the Blanched Soldier when, as you so aptly put it, Watson had deserted you for a wife.

Best wishes for the future,
                            Barbara Silver

P.S. Cocaine addiction is very bad for the mind. Please refrain from that lowly habit. B.S.


## Basil of Baker Street

*Nabnasset, Massachusetts, USA*
Dear Sherlock Holmes,

We liked the books that you wrote and our teacher read one of your books. The name of the book is *Basil of Baker Street*. It was real good, too. The whole class liked it. Thank you for the nice books that you wrote.

Your friend,
                            Sharry Westberg


## The Seven-Per-Cent Solution

*Lindenhurst, New York, USA*
Dear Mr Holmes,

I neither accept nor discredit your reality. Since it is easier for me, I will write this letter to you personally.

I have just finished reading the latest book about you, *The Seven-Per-Cent Solution*. One note, stay off cocaine! If Professor Moriarty doesn't kill you, it will. The book was excellent and I thoroughly enjoyed it.

Much continued success. Stay healthy and say hello to Dr Watson.

Yours truly,
                            Roy Hopp

## The Works of Arsène Lupin

*Yamaguchi-City, Japan*

Dear Sherlock Holmes,

I read your romances. They are very interesting. You solved many affairs. It is very splendid. You are very strong and bravery.

Do you know that Arsène Lupin wrote books? I read those books. Will you write books? I will read the books if you write them.

What are you doing now? Please take care of yourself.

Yours sincerely,
Haruko Uchimura

## Sherlock Holmes as Playwright

*Romulus, Michigan, USA*

Dear Sherlock Holmes,

I have read your play and I think it is a good play, and I thought that I would write to you and tell you that it was good.

Truly yours,
Polly Sudan

## The Broadway Melodrama

*Medford, New York, USA*

Honourable Mr Holmes,

My mother and father saw your play, *Sherlock Holmes*, on Broadway last week, but they said that it did not do you or Dr Watson justice.

I was hoping you would advise me if Dr Watson still assists you in solving cases, and can you tell me if Mr Moriarty is still at large?

My kindest regards and respect,

Morgan Munoz


## Star of the Silver Screen

Chicago, Illinois, USA

Dear Sherlock Holmes,

Are you still a movie star? I have never seen your movies, but many people have been talking about you. They say you make very good pictures. Would you put on another show for me, please.

Also, will you please send me a signed photograph that shows you just as you are in the newspapers? Thank you.

Sincerely,

Garrie Staback


## Two Great Films

Chelsea, Massachusetts, USA

Dear Sherlock Holmes,

I enjoy your films very much. I especially like, *Dressed to Kill* and *The Pearl of Death*. I hope you make some new ones.

Your best fan,

Debbie Blyth

P.S. Please say hello to Dr Watson and Mrs Hudson for me.

## The 'Silver Blaze' Film Script

Kitaadach-gun, Saitama-ken, Japan

Dear Sherlock Holmes,

I am your enthusiastic fan. Just after I read your film *Silver Blaze*, I found myself to be an enthusiastic fan – and I've read a lot of your books before. I cannot find the reason why I am so enthusiastic a fan, I cannot help being grateful to you for your inspiring me to open my eyes. I pray that you will be a successful player for a long time.

Goodbye, Mr Sherlock Holmes,

Yoshie Yoshida


## The Three Brothers

Elz, bei Limburg, West Germany

Dear Mr Sherlock Holmes,

I'm a fan of you. I think you are the best detective in the world. The films of you are on German TV. The film named *The Three Brothers*.
    Please send me a letter, and excuse me, my English isn't good.

Best greetings,

Jens Falk


## Sherlock Holmes and Dr Watson

Borgentreich, bei Warburg, West Germany

Mr Sherlock Holmes,

We are three German boys. Our name is Dirk, Detlef and Ralf. Our age is twelve, twelve and fourteen. Dirk and Detlef are brothers. Our English is not good. We are friends. We want three autographs.

We are watching the good film *Sherlock Holmes and Dr Watson*. We are become fans from Sherlock Holmes. We are reading books from Sherlock Holmes. Our love story is 'The Red Band'.

Loving,
> Dirk Kriegel, Detlef Kriegel, Ralf Uffelmann


## The Complete Sherlock Holmes

> *Milwaukee, Wisconsin, USA*

Dear Sir,

Every time I pick up my copy of *The Complete Sherlock Holmes* I feel the great detective is alive and well. His memoirs have been the best reading for a relaxed evening on many, many occasions.

Sincerely yours,
> Edwin A. Brylow


## Problems in Sherlockian Scholarship

> *Raleigh, North California, USA*

Dear Sherlock,

I am an avid fan of yours. I have read about all of your interesting feats of observation, but there are several points which still remain out of my grasp. For instance, whose gold watch was it that had been so mishandled? What was the book that Joseph Stangerson carried in his pocket? Why was Mycroft Holmes and the Diogenes Club heard of only once or twice? How was it that Dr Watson happened to cherish a portrait of Henry Ward Beecher, but had never had it framed? Why was Mrs Hudson never implicated in a mystery of her own? Why did Gregson and Lestrade gradually fade out of the picture? Why does

Billy, the page-boy, remain only a phantom? You speak once of having been to a college; which one was it? And Dr Watson's wound from the Jezail bullet; which was it in, the shoulder or the leg?

If you could answer any of these questions, I would be delighted.

Thank you,
Frank Gordon


# Sherlock Holmes at Fault

*London* SE 3

Dear Mr Holmes,

The stories written about you by A. Conan Doyle were – and are – marvellously entertaining; but as a detective, you were never more than a commonplace amateur and, I have to say, a showman or even a charlatan. You may have showed well in contrast with the fumbling police of your day; but you would have been quite outclassed by the best of the Bow Street Runners.

The stories in many cases are clearly pure fiction. I have tried writing on a wall with my finger dipped in copious quantities of poster-paint and it is quite impossible to produce a legible word within a period of twenty minutes; and, in that time, blood would have congealed to a near-solid mass.

You gave, it seems, much attention to footprints; but always in conditions where the operation was pointless. A gravel path, even at its muddy edge, can show no clear impression. Still less can a stair-carpet (after the front hallway had been walked on); and (in the case of the Admiralty clerk) your 'identification' of a wet shoeprint on the polished linoleum (after the person had walked up a flight of stairs and along a corridor) must surely have been a figment of a disordered imagination.

Any competent detective-inspector could easily show the numerous errors both in your reasoning and in your techniques for the apprehension of the miscreants. In this connection one is at a loss to understand why, having enlisted the aid of the police, you should always have taken it upon yourself to supervise what was purely their function and, indeed, why they ever permitted you to do so.

*The Hound of the Baskervilles* is, in my view, the best of the stories and surely the most entertaining. I am only thankful that I read it, saw an excellent film of it and heard a superb radio adaptation of it long before I realized that (a) no dog would ever pursue a person in such isolated circumstances where no 'intrusion' or 'threat' had taken place; (b) the stout boots of Sir Henry, cleaned every day, could not have left a strong-enough scent; and (c) as a dog has poor eyesight even in broad day, it would never have seen him in that mist. It would merely have padded around aimlessly.

Finally: I'm aware that 'Baker Street' itself was a piece of fiction for obvious reasons. My own deductions indicate either Tollington Park or Westbourne Terrace as your address. It could certainly *not* be in Baker Street w 1, which, then as now, was an expensive area and not a place in which persons of limited means could find an apartment with service. Also, of course, there were no lively urchins in w 1. I suggest that you make these facts clear to all the poor fools who write to you. *The truth shall make thee whole*; and we are bedevilled enough by fiction which purports to be fact.

Yours sincerely,
R. C. Hope

## The Speckled Bands

*Frankfort, Kentucky, USA*

Dear Mr Holmes,

After reading the reports of your 'Adventures of the Speckled Band', it has come to my attention that there may have been two different pet snakes kept by the abominable Dr Roylott; thus, please hear my reasons: The fact that Dr Roylott died 'within ten seconds' – whereas Julia Stoner 'slowly sank and died' – has led to the suggestion that Dr Roylott kept different snakes. By closely studying Indian snakes (because of Dr Roylott's frequent trips to Asia) you can easily see that the description may fit many varieties of serpents.

The band may have been the common Indian cobra (*Naja naja*); it may have been a viper, perhaps the ridge-scaled viper (*Echis carinata*). As you can see, there may have been more than one, because of the many different snakes with similar markings; as a result, I suggest that you return to the scene of the atrocity and search the grounds for another snake.

With due respect,
> Jim McGowan
> Private Detective

## The Hound of the Baskervilles

*Lawrenceburg, Indiana, USA*

Dear Mr Holmes,

I am enrolled in a Suspense Literature class in my high school. We have just finished *The Hound of the Baskervilles*, and I was wondering about a statement you made. You said that love and fear were by no means incompatible. Could you please write me and explain what you mean by this?

I would appreciate an answer to this letter as the problem is bothering me very much and I am at a loss for an explanation.

Sincerely,
> Jimmy Schaefer

## Stapleton's Motive

*Rheinbach, West Germany*

Dear Mr Holmes,

We know that you are not the true Holmes, but you know all about him and so we write to you. A pupil of our class has written a report about the book, *The Hound of the Baskervilles*. But we don't understand the motive of the murderer. Maybe you can explain this to us? We would be very thankful.

Sincerely,
        Elke Wetzig


## The Reigate Puzzle

*Dunwoody, Georgia, USA*

Dear Mr Holmes,

I have just finished reading 'The Reigate Puzzle' and was wondering if your dear friend, Dr Watson, was the originator of the phrase 'There is method in his madness'. Also, in this case story you were ill, what previous case had made you so ill? Have a good year!

Sincerely,
        Lynne Riley


## The Norwood Builder

*Fairfield, Connecticut, USA*

My Dear Mr Holmes,

Me and my friend have a question about 'The Norwood Builder'. What did Jonas put in the fire? You asked him what he had put in the fire, but he wouldn't tell you. You thought it was a rabbit. If that was so, how did it look like flesh?

Yours truly,
        Virginia Fodor

*Drawn by Sidney Paget.*

THE REICHENBACH FALLS.

Where it was thought that SHERLOCK HOLMES had met
with an untimely death.

# The Giant Rat of Sumatra

*The Jackson Laboratory, Bar Harbor, Maine, USA*

Dear Mr Holmes,

I am a pre-college student at the Jackson Laboratory and a great fan of yours. There are twenty-five of us students living here at Highseas and tonight the subject of the 'Giant Rat of Sumatra' came up at dinner. We all work with some highly genetically standardized inbred mice, but we know very little about rats in general. The programme here will be lasting only another two weeks and we would all really appreciate reading anything at all that you could send us about your giant rat.

The other kids think I'm insane for expecting a letter back from you. I think I remember reading in the *New York Times* that you are very good about answering mail. Please don't let me down.

Most sincerely yours,
Donna King

# [ 2 ]
# Friends and Associates

## Literary Genius

Dear Dr Watson,

I have often read your accounts of the cases of Mr S. Holmes. I greatly admire your literary genius. Please, will you send me a short note showing that you have acknowledged this letter. I would be most grateful.

Love from
         C. Fewson

## The Crown Prince of False Security

*Sacramento, California, USA*

Dear Dr Watson (or his appointed secretary),

I realize that you must be inundated with correspondence concerning your chronicles. I do not wish to impose upon your retirement serenity, however I do have a question concerning a statement supposedly made by Mr Holmes.

I am a college electronics instructor, and a student of mine informed me that Mr Holmes once said: 'Electricity is the crown prince of false security.'

The student said that Mr Holmes was referring to trust in burglar alarms (a new invention at the time), but I have not been able to locate the quote in your journals. Could you find the time to substantiate or refute the quote? I have my doubts as to its authenticity even though it has the ring of a product of Mr Holmes's wit.

Thank you for your consideration,

Morris T. Erickson

## From the Shingle of Deauville

Deauville, Normandy, France

My Dear Watson,

I am a little french boy who is eleven years and who spends his holidays at the seaside near Deauville.

I read your books and I am fond of them. You are a very grown-up detective with your friend Sherlock Holmes. Have you always many investigations in London and its suburbs? How do you do? Are you ill?

Here the sun always shines during the day. Is it like that in London? I swim in the sea because the weather is very hot.

I hope that this letter is well drawn up.

Yours sincerely,

Nicolas Lebon

## Dr Watson, Consulting Detective

Boise, Idaho, USA

Dear Sir,

Being the underdog in the Sherlock Holmes stories, I wonder how you feel having Holmes get all the credit? Wouldn't you like to get some credit for your help?

Wouldn't you like to solve a case by yourself for a change, instead of Holmes all the time?

Yours truly,
David Corringer

## The Raunheim Telegram

*Raunheim, West Germany*

DEAR HOLMES

GLAD TO HAVE CASE – YOUR ASSUMPTIONS WERE
RIGHT – JEWELS GONE – STATUE GONE – FORMULA
STOLEN – POLICE INCAPABLE – PROF. DR HANS MEIER
KIDNAPPED – ME TOO! – WHAT SHALL I DO? –
IMPATIENTLY AWAITING FURTHER INSTRUCTIONS –
(STOP)

WATSON

## The Solihull Interlude

*Solihull, Warwickshire*

Dear Sherlock,

This is your old pal, Watson, writing to see how you are getting on. How are Lestrade and Gregson of Scotland Yard? Is 221B still in good cop?

I've got to go now.

J. H. Watson

## The Essen Kidnap Note

*Essen, West Germany*

Dear Mr Holmes,

Herewith I inform you that I'll kidnap you and your friend, Dr Watson, next week. I would be very pleased if you agree to a ransom of £2.50 in stamps so that I needn't kidnap you.

If you won't give me the ransom, please tell me which food you like most.

Yours faithfully,
Arnd Mengeler

## The Abduction of Dr Watson

*Glucksburg, Ostsee, West Germany*

I've got your friend, Dr John Watson. If you want to see him alive again, send £5,000 sterling to my address.

Birgit Klinkowski

## The Further Reminiscences of John Watson, MD

*Covington, Kentucky, USA*

Dear Mr Holmes,

I have been a fan of yours for many years. I have read the short story, 'A Scandal in Bohemia'; a play *The Case of the Sussex Vampire*; and have seen the movies of 'The Final Problem', 'The Case of Five Orange

Pips', *The Hound of the Baskervilles*, 'The Case of Lady Penrose' and some more.

I hate to ask this of Dr Watson, but would you ask him to give me some more of your interesting cases and some newspaper clippings?

Thank you Mr Holmes and Dr Watson. Merry Christmas and a Happy New Year!

Truly yours,
David Gand


## Dr Watson's Middle Name

*New York, USA*

Dear Sir,

I would appreciate it immensely if you could answer a question of mine. I would like to know what the middle initial, 'H', in Dr Watson's name stands for; and does Sherlock Holmes have a middle name and if so, what is it?

I am yours very sincerely,
David Blaustein


## The Old Service Revolver

*Redhill, Surrey*

Dear Mr Sherlock Holmes,

Your medical colleague, Dr Watson, in his records of you, often mentions his service revolver. Why is he able to possess this when, as a Service Medical Officer – as with Service Chaplains – he should be unarmed?

Yours sincerely,
W. H. Bourne (Rev.)

## The Location of Dr Watson's Wound
## or the Mystery of the Jezail Bullet

*Fallowfield, Manchester*

Dear Sir,

I have finally decided to write to you about a matter that has puzzled me for some time, namely the location of Dr Watson's wound occasioned by the Jezail bullet.

In *A Study in Scarlet*, John H. Watson, MD, late of the Army Medical Dept, writes, 'I was struck on the shoulder by a Jezail bullet', whereas, when describing the Science of Deduction in *The Sign of Four*, he states, 'I sat nursing my wounded leg. I had had a Jezail bullet through it some time before'.

In later reminiscences the leg re-occurs, so I think that is the most likely area of the wound, but nevertheless I would appreciate fuller information on the matter.

Thank you for sparing me your time.

Yours faithfully,
Trevor Priestley


## Dr Watson's Figure

*Thomasboro, Illinois, USA*

Dear Sherlock Holmes,

My English class and I have been wondering if your friend, Watson, was fat or thin. Could you tell us?

Sincerely,
Lori Moran

*Drawn by Sidney Paget.*

" The Silhouette on the Blind was a perfect
reproduction of HOLMES."

Extract from *The Strand Magazine.*

# Was Watson a Woman?

*Cos Cob, Connecticut, USA*

Dear Mr Holmes,

I must excuse myself for this imposition on your time, but I have an important question. Was Watson a woman? I say he was not; a friend disagrees. Please reply to this urgent request.

May you live for ever, and not only 'in a romantic chamber of the heart, in a nostalgic country of the mind'. Thank you for your time.

Sincerely yours,
Cait N. Murphy


# The Problem of Dr Watson's Wife
## and the Fantastic Capabilities of Sherlock Holmes

*Bremen, West Germany*

Dear Mr Holmes,

About your fantastic capabilities of logical thinking and combination, I become enthusiastic always.

What has happened with the wife of Dr Watson? I don't remember to have read it.

I see in German TV cases which you have solved and I am very interested to have the address of the actor who plays your person. I believe that is a small matter for you, to send it me.

I shall be enjoyed when you will answer me.

Many greetings,
Petra Marquardt

## The Dying Doctor

*Mt Zion, Illinois, USA*

Dear Mr Holmes,

I wonder if you could tell me whether there is any truth in the rumour
that Dr Watson is fatally ill. Is he?

I also want to know the colour of his eyes.

Sincerely yours,
Mike Armstrong

## The Late John H. Watson, MD

*Haselan, West Germany*

Dear Sherlock Holmes,

I'm a fan from you and I want to have your signature and your photo,
please.

And now my question: Is Dr Watson dead or live he?

Question over. I hope you are writing me and send me the signature
and the photo.

Yours,
Frank Breitenseiter

## In Praise of Dr Watson

*Laurel Hill, Florida, USA*

Dear Mr Holmes,

I've been reading about you for years and I really disagree with you
on the point that Watson did a poor job. I really enjoy reading about
you – it sharpens my wits. I think Dr Mortimer isn't the only person

in the world who covets your skull, much as it might offend you to say so!

Can you tell me some things about yourself and Dr Watson? Better still, have you a picture of yourself? That really would be interesting as the illustrations in my books are poor.

Have a wonderful day!

Thank you,
Regina Harrison

## A Replacement for Dr Watson

*Springfield, Illinois, USA*

Dear Mr Sherlock Holmes,

I have written to congratulate you on your ability to solve cases.

I'm like Watson in the mysteries, not the great mind, but the one who looks for and seeks adventure. 'And that's elementary, dear Holmes, elementary!'

Sincerely yours,
Michelle Mulvey

P.S. If you ever need a new partner, just write to me. I'll be glad to help!

## Watsonian Empathy

*Asani-ku, Osaka, Japan*

Mr Holmes,

How do you do? I have read many books about you, but I don't get tired of them. I feel them very fresh every time I read them. When any complicated matter happen, you judge coolly and solve all riddle.

I always think I can do so. But one's character is controlled by nature, therefore I can't imitate what you do.

By the way, I feel familiar to you. When I read your story, I feel like I'm Dr Watson. I always become so. After I see the movies and read the books, I feel I'm with you in those.

Well, I like your own way. That looks like detective Colombo. Then I'm eagerly looking forward to the answering from you.

Yours truly,
Reiko Watabe

## The Two Collaborators
## Dr Watson and Dr Conan Doyle
~
### Sherlock Holmes in Canada

*Swisshome, Oregon, USA*

Dear Sir,

Could you tell me who wrote Sherlock Holmes. I hear it was Arthur Conan Doyle, but I have also heard that Dr Watson was the one. Did Dr Watson really live and did he team up with Arthur Conan Doyle to write about Sherlock's adventures? Also, was *The Seven-Per-Cent Solution* written by Dr Watson himself?

Could you tell me about Dr Watson's life and his part in Sherlock Holmes's life. Was there a case when Sherlock Holmes was in the United States and then in Canada; was there a case of 'The Lady in Green'?

Finally, could you tell me if there are any Sherlock Holmes fan clubs and how to join them.

Thank you,
John Kelly

# Sir Arthur Conan Doyle

*Louisville, Kentucky, USA*

Dear Sir,

I would like to get the physical description of Sir Arthur Conan Doyle: His height, weight, eyes, hair. Was he right or left-handed? And can you tell me how I can get a picture of him.

I've heard there is a Conan Doyle Museum in Switzerland. Can you tell me its address?

Thank you anyway,

Irvin Lush

# Mr Conan Doyle
## *of 221B Baker Street*

*Hamburg, West Germany*

Dear Mr Conan Doyle!

My name is André Haase. I'm thirteen years old and I have a great wish. Would you please send me an autogram from you? In the meantime I've got a lot of German film-stars and I should be very proud of getting an answer from England. Many thanks and greetings from

Yours sincerely,

André Haase

# Mycroft Holmes and Moriarty

*Calgary, Alberta, Canada*

Mr Holmes,

Although, as to date, I have not read a great number of your cases, the ones that I have read have been very enjoyable. A friend of mine who has read a great number tells me you have an older brother. Could you please tell me his name and what he does? Also, perhaps you could supply me with some information about yourself. And, who is 'Moriarty'?

Sincerely yours,

M. E. Fodchuk


# Professor Moriarty's Christian Name

*Baltimore, Maryland, USA*

Dear Mr Holmes,

I would like to ask you a few questions about yourself and your job. Then you could give me the answers by writing back.

The first question is about 'The Adventure of the Empty House'. What was Professor Moriarty's first name? Then, do you ever get scared solving some of the cases?

I love reading your books. Could you please tell me some of the books that you like and think I would like? Thank you so much.

Randee Venick

9 Eriswell Road,

Worthing.

18th Novr 1904.

Dear Sir,

I trust I am not trespassing too much on your time
and kindness by asking for the favour of your autograph
to add to my collection.

I have derived very much pleasure from reading
your Memoirs, and should very highly value the possession
of your famous signature.

Trusting you will see your way to thus honour
me, and venturing to thank you very much in anticipation,

I am, Sir,

Your obedient Servant,

*Charles Wright.*

P.S. Not being aware of your present address, I am taking
the liberty of sending this letter to Sir A. Conan
Doyle, asking him to be good enough to forward it to
you.

Sherlock Holmes Esq.

# The Reichenbach Substitution Theory

*Ivor, Virginia, USA*

Dear Mr Sherlock Holmes,

I have been a great admirer of yours for as long as I can remember. I have a large pipe collection (most of them Holmesian pipes) and many books about Watson and yourself and your adventures. My friend is also interested in you and your cases and is always asking me questions about you. We often play 'Holmes and Watson'. I am Holmes and I am a pretty good detective. I even have a Sherlock Holmes suit to play in.

But I have a question and I would be infinitely grateful to you if you would answer it. You see, I have a theory that the man you pushed over the falls at Reichenbach was not Professor James Moriarty, but a hired actor. Moriarty hired this actor because he knew there would be danger in your meeting. But you didn't learn this until you made your 'Return' in 1894. Is this theory true? If so, was he ever caught? Was he hanged or did he escape? If he escaped, did he die of natural causes? Did you ever meet up with him again?

Please answer. I am looking forward to your letter. Give my regards to Watson. To both of you, I am now as I ever was and forever shall be,

Very truly yours,

James Arrington

# Moriarty in America!

*West LaFayette, Indiana, USA*

Dear Mr Holmes,

Is it possible that Professor Moriarty escaped the Reichenbach Falls? I ask only because recently while passing through the municipal train station in Kansas City, a porter named James Moriarty assisted me with my luggage. This man was the very image of *the* Professor. In addition to this remarkable resemblance, many strange occurrences have in recent years caused much consternation within our local newspapers as well as in our law-enforcement agencies.

Could these series of heinous crimes have been perpetrated by Moriarty? Your considered opinion would be invaluable.

Sincerely,
James A. Cole


## The Napoleon of Crime

*Frankerthal, West Germany*

Dear Mr Holmes,

I have read many stories of you and Dr Watson, but today are so many books of you in the sale that I don't know what is true or what is invent. So I want to ask you whether Professor Moriarty, the Napoleon of Crime, is really dead. Have you actually tumble him into the Reichenbach Falls?

Is it true that you will retire?

Yours sincerely,
Jens Kersten

# The Purloined Paintings

Boston, Massachusetts, USA
Dear Sir,

I wonder if you have a small souvenir, of any kind, connected with your arch-enemy, Moriarty? I am a new Sherlock Holmes fan and it would be a great prize to show to other fans. Also, I wonder if you have been called in on the recent art thefts which have plagued Europe. And what has your distinguished biographer, Watson, been doing lately?

Ever truly yours,
Michael Kordis

# Moriarty, Mrs Hudson, and the Knighthood

Boothwyn, Pennsylvania, USA
Dear Mr Holmes,

I am well-acquainted with most of your cases. My favourite of these being the adventure at Baskerville Hall.

You and Dr Watson have thrilled me ever since Basil Rathbone and Nigel Bruce portrayed you in their films. As a long time enthusiast of your remarkable careers, I have a few questions for you to answer. I would be greatly pleased if you would do so.

1. Have you worked on any cases lately? If so, would you describe them for me?
2. What became of Moriarty?
3. Would you handle a case for anyone?
4. Is Mrs Hudson still living?
5. Is there a knighthood in your future?

Give my best regards to John and bless you.

Sincerely,
Christopher Roberts

# [ 3 ]
# Collectors

## Celebrated Calligraphy

*Chislehurst, Kent*

Dear Mr Holmes,

I am a great fan of yours and I am proud to say I have read every account of your work that has been written by Dr Watson. I have myself developed a power of deduction and have solved a few minor crimes, such as silver robberies.

But the reason I write is to ask a favour. I have for a long time collected literature about you, and a personal letter from you would be an ideal item for my collection. Therefore a letter of reply would be received with gratitude.

Yours,
Jonathan Ross

## The Mounted Memorial of Chicago

*Chicago, Illinois, USA*

My Dear Mr Holmes,

Please accept my heartfelt thanks for the endless hours of enjoyment you have provided. In 'Bohemia', as in all of your cases, you were remarkable. However, I feel the *Hound* brought to light the true level of genius you possess.

It is my understanding that I will hear from you at your earliest convenience. Your letter, of course, will be immediately framed and hung in my library.

Anxiously awaiting your reply,
Terry L. Nichols

# The Autograph of the Master

*Sioux Falls, South Dakota, USA*

Dear Mr Holmes,

I do not write to ask advice on any insoluble problem, but only to express my appreciation for many hours of pleasure in reading of your innumerable exploits.

As an avid fan of logical thought, I should be very grateful for an autograph of the last master detective and man of reason. Thank you very much.

Respectfully yours,
Dale Reed Hart

# A Famous Signature

*Skien, Norway*

Dear Sir,

I am a Norwegian boy, and one of my hobbies is collecting signatures of famous persons. I should therefore be very pleased if you would send me your personal signature.

Yours faithfully,
Fredrik Kittilsen

# Wilson, the Postcard Hunter

*Wandsworth, London* s w 1 8

Dear Sir,

Will you please send me a postcard signed by you. How is Watson?

Yours faithfully,
John Wilson

## A Cabinet Portrait

*Innsbruck, Austria*

Dear Sir,

Excuse me that I take up your precious time. I read many stories from you and so I would like to have a photo of you. If it is possible for you to send me one, I can only say thank you.

Yours faithfully,
> Georg Rock


## The Missing Caricature

*Staten Island, New York, USA*

Sirs,

You have always made a habit of helping those in need. My dilemma is within your boundless deductive powers. How may I complete my Holmes collection? Elementary! An autographed caricature – if possible in a personalized fashion.

Many thanks for countless hours of suspense and enjoyment. And regards to Dr Watson.

Yours truly,
> Adam Proios

# An Autographed Picture

The Art Institute of Chicago,
Chicago, Illinois, USA

Dear Mr Holmes,

Please send me an autographed photograph of yourself, plus some biographical information about your life and career.

I also would like information about joining your fan club, the Baker Street Irregulars. Please send me some information and addresses about it.

Thank you,
Sharon Lindy

# A Baskerville Nocturne

Charleston, West Virginia, USA

Dear Mr Holmes,

I have just about finished the book called *The Hound of the Baskervilles*. I found myself up at 10.30 at night reading. I was wondering if you happened to have any pictures of the inside of Baker Street or maybe a picture of the Moors (the only ones I have seen like the description given in the book are the Michigan Marshlands).

Yours truly,
Joe Hoffer

## The Letter from Edward Lear

*Cincinnati, Ohio, USA*

To Whom it may concern,

I understand that there is someone who answers requests to Mr Sherlock Holmes. Is there any chance that I may obtain some Holmes memorabilia?

In any case I would appreciate an answer.

Sincerely,
Edward Lear

## Baker Street Figurines

*Barnstaple, North Devon*

Dear Sherlock,

I have been an avid reader of your books since I was seven, and I think you are ace. My favourite novels, are *The Hound of the Baskervilles*, *The Sign of Four*, and *The Valley of Fear*; my favourite short stories are 'The Speckled Band' and 'The Five Orange Pips'.

Please could you send me, if possible, figures of yourself, Watson and Moriarty for my brother and I, and one of Mrs Hudson for my mum. If not, could you please send me a list of other souvenirs.

Yours sincerely,
Edward Gaughan

# The Badge Factory

*Stonyhurst, via Blackburn, Lancashire*

Dear Sherlock Holmes,

I like reading your books. I have got a book called *Ten Tales of Detection* which contains the story called 'The Adventure of Silver Blaze'. Could you send me a list of all the books with you in?

Please could you also send me a badge or something like that, and Sherlock Holmes's signature. If you have not got a badge, could you make me one with his signature on?

Yours sincerely,

Edward Foster-Knight


# Request for Buttons and Bumper Stickers

## With an Inquiry Concerning the Authenticity of *The Seven-Per-cent Solution*

*Mill Valley, California, USA*

Dear Sherlock,

I've heard that if someone writes to you in England, you will give them a reply. I want to know if *The Seven-Per-Cent Solution* by Nicholas Meyer is remotely authentic. I didn't think it was, but I want to know for sure.

Please send your answer to me along with any buttons, bumper stickers or Sherlock Holmes souvenirs that you have. Thank you very much.

Michael Elliott

# A Leningrad Letter

*Leningrad, USSR*

Dear Mr Sherlock Holmes,

It was very interesting for me to have read about your adventures written by Sir Arthur Conan Doyle. I admire your great talent to reveal the secrets of the crimes, your reliable method of the deductive analysis. Not long ago I have read in a newspaper about your home on Baker Street and I decided to write to you (or to your secretary). I collect stamps and postcards with the views of the interesting places and I would like very much to receive together with your answer some postcards with the views of the places connected with your name. In return I enclose some views of Leningrad. I will be very glad if you fulfil my request.

I thank you beforehand.

Yours sincerely,
Svetlana Shakova

P.S. Please give my best wishes to Dr Watson.


# Ex Libris

*Spakenburg, Holland*

Dear Mr Holmes,

I hope you're still alive. If so, you should be a very old man. Well, I have a rather strange request. I suppose you have all the books about yourself. I have most of them too, but I am still looking for a copy of *The Hound of the Baskervilles*. Do you have more than one copy of this book, and if so, could you miss one? I would be very glad to have one. Here in Holland it is very difficult to catch one in English. All costs I'll pay of course.

Thanking you very much in advance,

I remain,
K. Geuchies

## The Abbey House Brochure

*Mount Zion, Illinois, USA*

Dear Doctor,

Will you please send me an autographed booklet on the Abbey House. Thank you very much.

Sincerely yours,
Susan Knop

## Naci Gogo, the Turk

*Küçükköy, Istanbul, Turkey*

Dear Mr Sherlock Holmes,

I am a Turkish boy and I astonished your stories, but I never reading your books. I hear my father your name. I am very eager reading your books. I am look for your books everywhere, but I not found. I wonder if your books publish in Turkey. I am request if possible send to your books lists. If I makes mistakes I am sorry. I am desire good days.

Naci Gogo

## A Case of Identity

*Lakeside, California, USA*

Dear Sherlock Holmes,

Please send me an I.D. card so I can go around holding up people.

Thank you,
Richard Stark

# A Student of Criminology

*Offenbach/Bieber, West Germany*

Dear Mr Sherlock Holmes,

Could you please send me a tin of the special dust used to fingerprint?

My room has been searched during my absence for a few days. Unfortunately I can't lock my door, since it's not provided with any lock. If you have time, could you come here, please. Details concerning your fee will be later agreed upon. I would be very grateful to you if you could let me know your decision as soon as possible.

Thank you in advance.

Your
    Katja Schickedanz


# Dr Watson's Car

*Mantorp, Sweden*

Hello Sherlock Holmes!

Are you at home? Oh, that's very good that you are so. The point is that we are collecting numbers of cars, so we would like to know your number.

I think you get many letters so perhaps you could also send us some stamps. And can you tell us something about all your cases. May we be your penfriends?

Goodbye,
    Petra and Pernilla Calmerberg

# A Famous Person's Pig

*Putney, London* s w 1 5

Dear Mr Holmes,

I have been collecting drawings of pigs by famous characters for some time and have recently been advised that you might be willing to furnish me with a pig drawn by your good self.

If this is the case, I would be most grateful if you could oblige me by closing your eyes whilst drawing the pig and re-opening them to sign it.

If I am not being too presumptuous in asking this of you, I look forward to mounting your sketch on my wall amongst many others to await their eventual publication.

Yours sincerely,

Colin Black

# [ 4 ]
# Professional Inquiries

## The Master of Deduction

*Silver Spring, Maryland, USA*

My Dear Mr Holmes,

I am terribly intrigued, to say the least, with you and the marvellously ingenious techniques you employ in order to solve some of England's most baffling crimes.

The entire nine weeks of my English class has been dedicated to you, Mr Holmes, in order that we might study 'The Master of Deduction'.

My class would be most honoured if you could see fit to visit our school and serve as a speaker with great personal knowledge. Your speech would stimulate and encourage those with potential in the crime-solving field.

I will wait most anxiously for your reply. I do sincerely hope that you will be able to make it. I am sure that you will find it most enjoyable.

Very sincerely yours,

Sue Nachman

## The Silver Spring Summons

*Silver Spring, Maryland, USA*

Dear Mr Holmes,

In one of our classes we are reading mostly about detective stories. We are great fans of yours and enjoy your novels and short stories tremendously.

If possible, Mr Holmes, we would like very much for you to visit our class. We know you are busy and may not be able to come, but could you possibly send a representative, perhaps Dr Watson? We will be glad to pay the fare and would be more than willing to do so.

If no one is available at this time, would you please send an autographed picture of yourself and anything else you may send to your admirers. We would appreciate it very much.

Sincerely yours,
      Brenda Spaid

## The Coleman Speech Suggestion

*Coleman, Oklahoma, USA*

Mr Holmes,

We, the Freshman Class of Coleman High School, have read quite a few of your stories and have become great fans of yours. We would like to know if you would come and give a talk about your stories to us. Our teacher said it would be just fine if you could come. If you can, could you make it around September? We would appreciate it very much, and I'm sure we'd all enjoy it. Thank you very much.

Sincerely yours,
      The Freshman Class of Coleman High School

## Holmes's International Detective Agency

*Baltimore, Maryland, USA*

Dear Mr Holmes,

I hope that you had a nice Christmas and did not have to work too hard over the holiday.

Would you ever consider coming to America and opening a business here? America is full of interesting crimes. We really could have used you in the Watergate case and the Patty Hearst case. Maryland has a lot of important cases and you are well respected here. There is even a Mr Holmes who owns a winning sailboat named 'Sherlock'.

In America we have some good science laboratories which you could use to mix up some new solutions. If you ever decided to sell some of them, you could find a big buying market.

Please let me know if you would like to move here. If you don't want to leave England, you could open up an American branch with assistants who could send you the facts so you could solve the cases. America could really use a good detective like you. You could even star in a television show.

Sincerely,
Claire Skarda

## The Rosedale Crickets Letter

Rosedale, New York, USA

Dear Mr Holmes,

I was wondering if you could take a boat and come to my school when school starts next month. It is very easy to get to and you can eat in the lunch room if you get hungry. You can share my room if you like. I have not asked my mother if you can but, since you are a famous detective, you can make her happy by finding her missing French cookbook. My room is warm and I have an extra bat so you can play with crickets (England's national pastime). I have a big Sony colour television set so you can watch your show, 'Sherlock Holmes Mystery Theatre', if you like. Please bring Dr Watson and the Hound of the Swamps. Dr Watson can sleep in my parents' room and look at sore throats, and the Hound of the Swamps can sleep in the swamps which are only three blocks away.

Please write me so I can meet you when your boat docks.

Hope you can get here soon,
John Cimisi

# The Rich Student of Loffingen

*Loffingen, West Germany*

Dear Sherlock Holmes!

We have a very nice English teacher. She read one of your detective-stories, *The Hound of the Baskervilles*, with us. So my friend and I got the idea to write you.

You most probably won't come to Germany, where we come from, as it's too expensive for you. So we ask you to send us some tips, how we can find out something about our English teacher (the age, for example).

If you can't give us any tips, we would be glad to get an answer.

Sincerely yours,
Georg Herbstritt


# The Laborde Document

*Oloron, France*

Dear Mr Sherlock Holmes,

I have recently read one of your books, *The Baskerville Dog*. The inquest was wonderful and quite exciting. I congratulate you!

But have you unravelled a new mystery recently? Why do you never come to France? You are very famous here and lots of French people think you could come and solve many problems.

What are your hobbies? And where's Mr Watson now? Does he still live with you? Can you send me an autograph and a recent photograph of you?

I would appreciate a prompt answer.

Yours sincerely,
Beatrice Laborde

# The Church of Scientology

*Church of Scientology, AOSH-UK, Saint Hill Manor*
*East Grinstead, Sussex*

Dear Mr Holmes,

You are invited to come to Saint Hill for a free Case Analysis. So do take advantage of this special offer to you at this time.

Best wishes,
Audrey White
Letter Registrar


# The Sign of the Two

*Tallahassee, Florida, USA*

Dear Sherlock Holmes,

I'm an eight-year-old detective named George Evans Light. I haven't read one of your books, but my friend and I have many clubs. Our sign is **FE** .

I'm engaged in a lot of spying and I've written a book about it. Here is one of my codes: A = 26, B = 25, C = 24 ... Z = 1.

Please send me your autograph and ways to solve mysteries. I would also like to take courses by mail on how to be a better spy.

Yours truly,
George Evans Light

P.S. When I come to London this July, I'll visit you.

# A Student of Disguise

*Albany, New York, USA*

Dear Sherlock Holmes,

I like detectives very much. I have played cops, spies, detectives and other games, but I have enjoyed playing detectives and spies the most. I like you and James Bond the most.

I play a lot of games, one day one thing, another thing another day. You too must have played many real detective games in your career.

I have a club of my own. Sometimes members of the club help other people and sometimes we help you and Watson. Unfortunately I am too tall to be a midget and too short to be a man, so I can not use disguises like beards, moustaches, and sideburns (all fake, of course). I would like to know some disguises I could use. I would really like to hear from you and John Watson.

Sincerely yours,
Timothy Keneally

# The Softer Passions of a Sherlockian

*Chillicothe, Montana, USA*

Dear Mr Holmes,

I have been an admirer of yours for years. I have read all the available stories about you. When I was younger, I bought a 'Sherlock' pipe, my nickname was Sherlock, and I said that whenever I grew up I wanted to be a detective and live in London.

Now that I am older and will soon graduate and then get married, I decided I should write to you and tell you that I am one of your many fans.

If I receive a reply from you, I plan to keep it with my books containing stories of you and show it to any children I give birth to or adopt.

Always an admirer,
Jennifer Emerich

P.S. I also think that you would make an enjoyable husband or lover for someone.

## Mute Inglorious Milton

*Milton, Ontario, Canada*

Dear Mr Holmes,

I have just started to read your books and I am enjoying them very much. I expect to be a detective when I get a bit older. We don't have too much crime in Canada, but when we do I will ask them to have you help to solve the case.

You are very lucky to have Mr Watson to help you. I also think he is a very lucky fellow.

I have visited London and liked it very much. I wasn't reading your books then or I am sure I would have liked to visit you.

I am eleven years old and live in the country. There is no one of my age living near by, so I read a lot and enjoy playing pool with my father and sometimes my mother.

Best regards to you and Mr Watson,

Rob Lewis Adams

## Some Village Hamden

*Hamden, Connecticut, USA*

Dear Mr Holmes,

I am one of your most beloved fans in the world. Some day I hope to be as good a detective as you. I'm thirteen years old and I live in Hamden, Connecticut. My town is a small one.

For Halloween I am going to play the part of Dracula! I'm renting the costume from the prop shop.

Will you please send me a picture of you and your pipe. That's all for now, but I'll write later.

Your friend,

David Johnson

## The Science of Deduction

*Budelsdorf, West Germany*

Dear Mr Holmes,

I have read the most of your stories. In the next year I get out of school and my greatest desire is to become a famous detective, as famous as you. I want to be the best, but if someone wants to be the best he must teach by the best.

Would you please teach me all that I must know to become a good detective?

I would be a great help for you and I learn fast. You wouldn't get any trouble with me. Please answer quick.

Yours faithfully,
Olaf Lipinski

P.S. Please forgive my bad English, but I learn every day, and in two months I will speak it perfectly.


## Joe Mannix and the Baker Street Maid

*Cornell, Illinois, USA*

Dear Mr Holmes,

I am quite interested in being a detective. I have read a lot of your mysteries and have enjoyed them all. In the case of the 'Sussex Vampire', why wouldn't the arrow have been empty of poison when it was bought in South America? And did Jacky change after going off to be a cabin boy? If so, how did he change, or is he still jealous of his little brother?

How is your maid, Mrs Hudson? Does she help you on any cases. And if so, how?

Do you know Joe Mannix? Do you think Joe is a good detective? If so, why, or if not, why? Do you know a lot of lady detectives? Would you please give me a few tips on being a good detective. I would appreciate your help very much.

Would you please send me a photo of Dr Watson and you. I would appreciate a picture very much.

Sincerely yours,
Susan Burkett

# The Lost Clues of Connecticut

*Fairfield, Connecticut, USA*

Dear Mr Holmes,

I'm trying to become a detective but every time something is missing in my house, it's just because someone lost it! If something is stolen, I can never get a suspect.

Could you please give me a few ideas on how to look for good clues and how to make a suspect show himself?

Sincerely,
John Fox


# The American Apprentice

*Portland, Oregon, USA*

Dear Mr Holmes,

I have enjoyed reading about your many adventures as a detective.

I would like to be a detective too, someday when I get bigger. Do you think this is a good idea for somebody who lives in the United States? We have many evil people here like you do in London.

Please write to me when you have some time between cases. I would like your opinion of investigation as a career.

Sincerely,
John W. Lee

P.S. I have a friend who would also like to hear from you. She wants to visit you when she goes to London.

# The Art of Detection

*St Edward's University, Austin, Texas, USA*

Dear Mr Holmes,

I am thinking of pursuing a career as a consulting detective. I have
read Dr Watson's accounts of your cases and admire you very much.
What advice would you give to a young person considering this line
of work? I respect your opinion and will appreciate any information
which you care to send. Thank you.

Sincerely,
> Kimberly Hemphill


# The Practical Handbook
## for the Identification of Clues
### or the Clue Manual

*Sahaurita, Arizona, USA*

Dear Sherlock Holmes,

I live in Sahaurita, Arizona. Some day I would like to be a great
detective like you.

I think it would be neat if you could send me a brochure or some
books on different kinds of clues.

Thank you for your help.

Sincerely,
> Matt Wright

# Professional Pointers

*Portland, Oregon, USA*

Dear Sirs,

Having been for many years an avid admirer of your writings and work, I wish to take this opportunity to thank you for the hours of enjoyment received and for the innumerable 'pointers' I have learned and applied to my work as investigator.

I would be thrilled to hear from you, should you find the time.

Cordially,
        J. E. Bouton

# The Solved Problem Carton

*Amado, Arizona, USA*

Dear Sir,

I'm a twelve-year-old that likes to solve easy problems of my own. I have a box of solved problems.

It would be wonderful if you could send me some advice on how to do detective work. Can you tell me how you're doing on the case you're on? And maybe I can help you on it. Thank you for your co-operation.

Sincerely,
        Sandy Vargas

## The Tokyo Entreaty

*Bunkyo-ku, Tokyo, Japan*

My Dear Mr Holmes,

I'm a private detective and I have cleared up many mysterious affairs, but the affair which I investigate now is so difficult. It's out of my hand. So I have a favour to ask of you. I hear that you are one of the best detectives in the world. Would you mind coming to Japan to help me?

Thank you in anticipation.

Yours truly,
Kogoro Akechi

## The Last Resort

*Newark, Delaware, USA*

Dear Sherlock,

There have been some very queer robberies going on. A valuable pearl necklace has been stolen from old widow Dixon. I'm a private detective, working like crazy on the case, something like the Hardy boys and 'all that rot' you might say. It looks as if nothing can be done, so I resorted to you, you old rascal!

What can you do?

Sincerely yours,
Robert Connin
Private Detective

# [ 5 ]
# Case Histories

## The Oklahoma Offer

Oklahoma City, Oklahoma, USA
Dear Mr Holmes,

Our office is most interested in engaging your services in reference to one of our clients. Please advise if you are available and we will proceed from that point.

I have the high honour to remain, Sir,

Your obedient servant,

Robert D. Norris, Jr
Attorney at Law

## The Montclair Inheritance Mystery

Montclair, New Jersey, USA
Dear Mr Holmes,

Forgive me for violating the solitude of a well-earned retirement, but I am at my wits' end over a matter that is both sinister and bizarre. I dare not give particulars here, for this letter must pass through several hands before reaching the safe stewardship of the United States Post Office. A small fortune in gold coins and the good name of a kindly South American heiress hang in the balance. It is enough to say that you have never had a greater opportunity to substantiate the claim made that you are the world's pre-eminent reasoner.

Please don't delay a moment. Even now events take a menacing shape. Your prompt reply will win my undying gratitude.

Yours faithfully and forever,

Charles Richard Furlong

# The Adventure of the Noble Family

*Tuart Hill, Western Australia*

Dear Mr Holmes,

I have read of your skill in detective work and believe you to be a man of discretion and intelligence. I require a confidential and exceptionally able agent in a particular matter concerning a certain noble family.

Would you please communicate with me a suitable time to call to discuss this matter with you.

I look forward to your reply with interest.

Yours faithfully,
D. Sutherland-Bruce

# The California Romance Case

*Fremont, California, USA*

My Dear Mr Holmes,

I am a young attorney in the wilds of California. I am working on a case now that needs all of the investigative tools of an ingenious mind such as yours.

Briefly I can tell you that it involves a young woman and love. I can explain nothing more until I receive your assurance that you have time to spare me.

Sincerely,
R. Lange

## The Pawtucket Problem

*Pawtucket, Rhode Island, USA*

Dear Mr Holmes,

I have admired your work as an exponent of the art of the consultative detective for a period of quite some years. I have been informed of late that you have chosen to retire to Sussex to engage in the raising of bees. This letter has been addressed to 221B Baker Street in the hopes that it will somehow reach you and that you will have the time and inclination to respond to my request for assistance in a matter of no small importance and regard to myself. I expectantly await the pleasure of your reply.

    With warmest regards,

                Paul Dobish, Jr

## The Cornwall-on Hudson Confidence

*Cornwall-on-Hudson, New York, USA*

Dear Mr Holmes,

I would like to contact you on business of a most confidential and dangerous nature. Only you can help me as Shaft and Mannix have already turned me down. Please contact me at once.

    Sincerely,

                Robert A. Burger

# Jack the Ripper

*Thousand Oaks, California, USA*

Dear Mr Holmes,

Your mysteries are interesting to me. I would like to have your answers to these few questions I have. What do you think about Jack the Ripper? Has he attempted any more murders? Is he still alive? Will you ever investigate any of his cases?

Thank you for your time. Looking forward to hearing from you.

Sincerely,
Mike Spurling

# The Watergate Affair

*Philadelphia, Pennsylvania, USA*

My Dear Mr Sherlock Holmes,

We have read Dr Watson's account of *A Study in Scarlet*, and we are fascinated by your ability to solve crimes. Would it be possible for you to assist in the Watergate investigations in our country?

Thank you for any help you can give us on this matter and we look forward to hearing from you and Dr Watson in the near future.

Very sincerely yours,
Geoffrey Snyder, Steve Guyer, Todd O'Neill, Andy Topping, Thomas Ferrell, Reginald Royster, Laurence Olivieri, Art Smithy, Gerald Crocker, Walter La Mar, Fernando L. Allende, Chucky Davis, Bob Parson, P. A. Biron, Peter Barston, James G. B. Perkins

P.S. Our best to Inspector Lestrade.

# A Scandal in America

Baltimore, Maryland, USA
Dear Mr Holmes,

We are encountering a mystery in our country well calculated to test even your great powers of deduction, if, of course, you find time to aid us.

It is called: 'I remember Watergate but somethings I can't recall, am in doubt about or at present don't know if my recollection is correct!'

Could you possibly come to our nation's capital and put the 'Nix' on the whole squalid affair?

Even if your busy schedule does not permit you to, your reply to this plea will always be treasured as it will be proof that I did everything possible to aid my country in its time of need.

Thank you,
Tom Kemp


## The Case of the Papers of Ex-President Nixon

Arvada, Colorado, USA
Dear Holmes,

I would like to talk to you sometime on the subject of Watergate. I think you could easily solve it with your sidekick Watson.

Also, if you would, could you or Watson write me a note explaining your supposed death at the hands of Professor Moriarty?

Your devoted fan,
Nick Gill

# The Howard Hughes Stock Case

*Alice, Texas, USA*

Dear Sherlock Holmes,

Could you come to the United States and help prove if Howard Hughes is dead or alive? My father owns some stock in Air West and would like to have the matter cleared up. There will be a large reward for your efforts.

Sincerely yours,
Alan Howard

# The Disappearance of Miss Patricia Hearst

*Ferndale, Michigan, USA*

Dear Mr Holmes,

I must be honest and tell you I am not a great fan of yours, although I have heard a lot about your success at solving mysteries.

I don't know if you are familiar with this case, in spite of it being nationally known. The story is that of a young girl, Patricia Hearst, who was kidnapped some months ago. For other information your best bet would be to contact Randall Hearst in Los Angeles.

So, Mr Holmes, if you would like to gain a lot of new fans and readers, I suggest you explain this mystery. No one but you, maybe, can solve it. Thank you.

A concerned American,
Therese M. Smith

To Sir Conan Doyle, Bart.

Will "Mr Sherlock Holmes"
require a housekeeper for
his country cottage at Xmas"
I know some one, who loves
a quiet country life, and
'Bees' especially. — an old
fashioned quiet woman

Yours faithfully.

M Gunton

To The Hon. P. Cranstoun
Hurst Hill House
Totland Bay
I of Wight.—

10 Oct 1904.

# The Patty Hearst Trial

*Springfield, Illinois, USA*

Dear Mr Sherlock Holmes,

We have been reading different stories about you, such as 'The Red Death' and 'The Speckled Band'. I really liked the way you figured those cases out.

I've got a case for you. The Patty Hearst trial is always in the news; they can't seem to figure out if she is guilty or innocent. They are trying her for a bank robbery after she was kidnapped by the CIA.

Maybe you have heard about it. She never came back even after the ransom was paid. She was gone for two years and then her group was caught. She is on trial now, but they can't find an answer. I wish you would help.

Yours truly,
> Brad Willey

# The Hoffa Case

*Ferndale, Michigan, USA*

Dear Mr Holmes,

I have a case for you. It's about our Teamster Leader, Mr Hoffa. He has been missing six weeks. His son thinks he's dead. But there is not enough evidence against anybody for a trial. I am writing to you because I know you can solve it or give me the clues.

Sincerely yours,
> John Repke

# Pirates of the Air

*San Jose, California, USA*

Dear Mr Holmes,

I want to know why you have not been called in to stop this terrible high-jacking [*sic*]. I travel by plane each week and would like your help in this matter. I think you are the only one who can stop this kind of thing. The high-jacking of airplanes must be stopped. Only you can do it.

Your friend,
R. L. Daniel


# The Lost Citizens
# of San Antonio

*San Antonio, Texas, USA*

Dear Mr Holmes,

Your name was given to me by a friend, although I had heard of you before. As I do not know your address I am asking a member of my family who lives in England to forward this to you.

In the past two years three people have disappeared in mysterious circumstances in San Antonio. The police treat them as separate investigations, but I am convinced that they are linked in some way. My theories are discounted because I have no professional standing, but if you were to look at the case I am sure that you would confirm my suspicions.

I urge you to contact the San Antonio police and offer your services. As they are quite baffled by the whole case I am sure that they would engage you immediately.

Yours sincerely,
Mike Chafetz

## The Terror of the Northern Regions
## or the Adventure of Black Mole

*Coventry*

Dear Mr Holmes,

I write to ask if you, the only man left in England with the ability to get to the bottom of murders, would undertake to seek out and put asunder the murderer of my auntie Anastasia – I mean of course the Accursed Black Mole of the Northern Regions.

Mr Holmes, I make no buts, but rest assured £250 in gold sovereigns will be yours if you find out this scoundrel.

I remain, &c, &c,

Ernie Hateman

## The Karlsruhe Lift Mystery

*Army Post Office, New York, USA*

Dear Mr Holmes,

Would you help me solve the mystery which occurred when my family went to Karlsruhe? We were in a large hotel and, after packing, I came down in the elevator with a friend. My parents and my brother came down next. The elevator got stuck and there was banging inside. The manager got his men to fix it, but there was nobody in there. Where could they be? Can you help me?

Sincerely,

Sylvia Zachary

# The Misplaced Sister

*Exton, Pennsylvania, USA*

Dear Sherlock,

Please help! My only sister has been missing for two weeks. Do you think you can find her? We have looked everywhere she might have gone, but no luck. The police have filed a missing-persons report but I don't think that will help. It seems like she has just disappeared off the face of the earth.

If this is not a problem for you I can hire someone else. I thought you were the best detective around so I picked you. I hope you can find her and return her to me.

Here are the facts that I think you will need. She was last seen leaving school on December 1. She is 5′ 4″ and weighs approximately 98 pounds. She has blond hair and hazel eyes. She was wearing brown corduroys and a beige sweater.

All her family and friends miss her greatly and hope you can return her safely to me. If you come up with any further clues, please contact me.

Sincerely,
    Jill Shoemaker


# The Takin Spell-Chamber

*Takin, Kansas, USA*

Dear Sir,

I hope you can help me with this case for I am very troubled. My uncle has completely disappeared and nobody has been able to locate him. He disappeared August 25th, while he was doing a magical show, and nobody can find him. Please reply and help me if you can.

Yours sincerely,
    Robin Duncan

## The Tired Uncle

Port Washington, Wisconsin, USA

Dear Mr Holmes,

Having been a devoted fan of yours for many years and having
followed your exploits with nothing less than an addiction, I now find
it necessary to write to you to ask for help. It concerns my missing
nephew who has supported me and been the only joy of my old age.

Lord knows, I have tried all avenues of approach to locate the boy,
but all the attempts have failed. So, having exhausted the regular
means, I am putting my plight before you for your most worthy
consideration. If you could but take the small bit of time necessary to
locate my twenty-year-old nephew and bring him back in touch with
me, it would heap upon you my greatest thanks. Please inform me
of your decision in this matter as it will mean a great deal to an old
man.

Awaiting your reply, I remain,

G. M. Murphy

## The Lost Farmington Friend

Farmington, Connecticut, USA

Dear Mr Holmes,

Due to your amazing reputation and your ability at solving even the
most hopeless cases, I am writing to ask for your help in finding a very
good friend of mine. He disappeared on the evening of January 1st
after visiting my home. He drove away at about 8 pm and hasn't been
seen or heard of since. His car was found two blocks from Main Street
apparently untouched and locked up tight.

The police have checked into the matter and to date have done little
beyond putting his name on their 'missing persons' list. I realize

that you are a very busy person, but as I see it you are my only hope of ever finding my friend.

Your answer by return mail would be greatly appreciated.

Very truly yours,
                    Mark Dipinto


## The Belgian Pit Mystery

*Musson, Belgium*

Dear Sherlock Holmes,

Two years ago my friend disappeared in the forest. The police searched everywhere but didn't find any trace of him. Then one day an archaeologist came to the village and went down one of the mines. He discovered a bag and a string belonging to my friend. At that moment everyone thought they were going to find the body, but they searched without success. From that day the disappearance of my friend has remained a mystery. That's why I ask you to help me. I think you are the only man who can solve this problem, and I need to know what happened to my friend.

Yours faithfully,
                    Martine Berque


## The Preceptor of Section 7C5

*West Chester, Pennsylvania, USA*

Dear Mr Holmes,

Many things around our school have vanished mysteriously. Small things like calculators and book-carts have disappeared. We did not pay too much attention to these losses. After a long weekend, we returned to school to find that the flags in each classroom had disappeared. There was no sign of a break-in.

That night, our English teacher stayed late. The next day, we returned to school to find that she was gone, but the strange thing was to see all her belongings in the room with the lights on. Her car was in the parking lot and there was no sign of forced entry and no sign of a struggle. She has been missing for three weeks.

We are sincerely upset by the loss of our teacher and we would truly like to have our school's possessions returned. We would appreciate your help to straighten out this case.

Sincerely,
The Students of Section 7c5

## *The Voyage of the* Darke

*Army Post Office, New York, USA*

Dear Mr Holmes,

Last week my friend was sailing in his boat, the *Darke*. We have not found him yet, but you are so brave and great that I thought you could go swimming in the middle of the Atlantic Ocean where he said he was going.

When you find him, send me two pictures of you and my friend together. One for me and one for his parents so they know he is safe.

Your friend,
Daniel Parlette

## The New Jersey Clam-Boat Tragedy

*Stone Harbor, New Jersey, USA*

Dear Mr Holmes,

As you have solved many difficult cases, I felt that you would be interested in a recent New Jersey mystery in which three young men disappeared from a clamming boat. As of today their bodies have not been found.

Perhaps you have an explanation? Your opinion will be held in high esteem.

Ever faithful,
Otto Emerson

## The Miller High Life Mystery

*Milwaukee, Wisconsin, USA*

Dear Holmes,

Visiting the Breweries in Milwaukee. A most interesting case has come up. A poor chap was found floating in one of the brewing kettles with the following insignia on his forehead ' ❦ '.

Hope to hear from you about this. Say 'hi' to Watson.

D. Devan

## The Quincy Theft Question

*Quincy, Massachusetts, USA*

Dear Mr Holmes,

I am very grateful to you because of the way you found those embezzlers in my firm in Quincy, but once again trouble has come to my firm. Here is the story.

On June 28th I was in my office at the plant when suddenly I heard a loud crash. I rushed out only to find that my safe was open and five thousand dollars were missing.

I have no idea what the crash was and the police have dropped the case. I am in desperate need of your help, please come as soon as possible.

Sincerely yours,
Matthew Macleod


## The Episode of the Empty Grain Barrels

*Richardson, Texas, USA*

Dear Mr Holmes,

I have read all your mysteries and know that a man with such an analytical mind as your own will be able to solve a mysterious and bizarre crime that has plagued my family.

My father owns a sheep and livestock farm forty miles north of where we live. For the past several months two or three heads of sheep have disappeared each night. The local police have been unable to solve this crime which shows no sign of stopping or subsiding. A few months ago several hundred of my father's empty grain barrels were stolen along with about twenty-five bales of hay. That was when the sheep started disappearing. Soon after, my father hired guards to keep watch over the farm at night and to keep a watch on the river that runs through the farm. Despite these precautions and keeping the sheep in locked barns, the disappearances continue. The only other structures on the farm, besides the barns and the workers' quarters, are three old oil rigs, the last remnants of an abandoned oil-field, in the western corner of the farm. The same men who worked for the now-bankrupt oil company are employed by my father, but they are to be trusted.

My family has lived the past few months in anguish. They are full of hope that you can help us, for no one else has been able to. Thank you.

Sincerely,
Tom Gehrlein

163

# The Staid Waiter

*Mesquite, Texas, USA*

Dear Mr Holmes,

I have heard that you are the greatest detective who ever lived. I am not sure if you would take a simple theft case and, if so, that I could afford your rates.

I work in a restaurant where a good deal of food and money is taken each week. As yet, we have not been able to catch the crook.

Do you handle cases such as this? And, if so, what would be the cost? Please reply soon and give me some idea as to what to do.

Sincerely,
Ralph B. Smith

# The Paris Incinerator and Siphon Mystery

*Paris, Illinois, USA*

Dear Sir,

We have been plagued by numerous mysteries at our home. Gas has been siphoned from my father's car in the yard and money and other invaluables have disappeared. Once we had a case where $20 came up missing without a trace, and then $13 addressed to my father turned up in our incinerator with an old letter of my mother's that was written to her twenty-one years ago.

I once had the culprit cornered in the hedge, but he eluded me. I have seen what appeared to be people running through our alley one at a time.

I have no answers although I have tried uselessly. Please answer me as I am desperate.

Sincerely,
Victor A. Valente

## The Illinois Blanket Business

*Springfield, Illinois, USA*

Dear Sherlock Holmes,

I have a case for you, my aunt's valuable vase was stolen. Since the theft, other objects have been taken; a salt-shaker, a book of crossword puzzles, a blanket and a thirty-foot rope. The theft of these things puzzled me, but I think they are connected with the stolen vase. Could you help me solve this crime?

Yours truly,

John Kunz


## *The Case of Mason Spencer Weiss*

*Rockville, Maryland, USA*

Dear Mr Holmes,

I would very much like to retain your services to locate some property of mine which disappeared under the most mysterious circumstances.

Please advise me at your earliest convenience if you will be able to handle my case. I know that only someone with your keen mind and deductive powers will be able to assist me.

Very truly yours,

Mason Spencer Weiss

366/AR.
England
Mr Sherlock Holmes
Detective Policeman
at
London
SW
R
London F. S.
R No. 10520

# The Dillsburg Gas Chamber

*Dillsburg, Pennsylvania, USA*

Dear Mr Holmes,

I urgently need your help in solving one of the most inexplicable and dastardly crimes ever to sweep the continent of North America.

I am a Rolls-Royce automobile collector. My entire collection is valued at five million dollars. Each week one of my precious cars is stolen. So far, nine cars have been taken.

At the scene of each crime there is a strong smell of ammonia and a reddish-coloured gas that fills the air. I have all my cars locked up in a steel garage.

Besides that, I have fifteen guards on duty round the clock, but they claim that there is no one entering or leaving the garage at any time . . .

I desperately need your help in this matter, Mr Holmes.

Sincerely,
    Michael Fuss

# The Singular Affair of the Aluminium Ball

*Pittsburg, Pennsylvania, USA*

Dear Mr Holmes,

I hope you can help me with a small but important problem. Being of a nervous disposition, several years ago I was ordered by my doctor to take up a relaxing hobby. As I am competitive by nature I selected an unusual hobby which could not easily be duplicated.

I hope you will not laugh when I tell you my hobby is collecting pieces of aluminium foil which I roll into a ball. Well, Mr Holmes, you can guess what has happened. My foil ball got so big that my wife insisted I get it out of the house. For a while I kept it in the garage, but eventually it got too crowded in there. Finally I was forced to roll the ball out into the yard, where because of the many nasty children in my neighbourhood, I had to chain my ball of foil to a tree.

Yesterday the ball disappeared!

True to your careful methods of pure, deductive reasoning, Mr Holmes, I was able to follow the ball's progress across the lawn because of the two smashed fences, remnants of a doghouse and a crushed Japanese car left in its wake. However, I lost its track in the street.

I have checked with all the metal recycling centres in my neighbourhood, to no avail. Obviously, some fiend has made off with my foil ball for some foul purpose too devious for the decent, ordinary mind to unravel.

I find this all very upsetting. I do hope you can find the time to look into this small matter, Mr Holmes, I shall be most worried until the whereabouts of my ball of foil is known and the perpetrator of the deed discovered.

Yours truly,
Peter Wainwright


# The Adventure of
# the Cardboard Box

*La Verne, California, USA*

Dear Mr Holmes,

I put my tooth in a cardboard box and now it's gone, so I'm asking you if you could help me. I would really appreciate it if you could send a letter back.

Your friend,
Deanna Wigert

## The Tooth of Gold

*Furth, West Germany*

Dear Sherlock Holmes!

I can't find my denture. I think it was stolen last night. It's golden and so it's a big loss. Please, Mr Holmes, come and find my denture, or give me some tips to find it.

Yours,
        Frederic Kormuth

P.S. If it's possible, could you answer in German, or easy English?

## The Demon Barber of Aitrach

*Aitrach, West Germany*

Dear Mr Sherlock Holmes,

Master, yesterday when I got to a hairdresser he have stealed from me simply a pair of hairs! Say me what that I do to get back my hairs, please.

                                                    Peter Mayer

## The Matter of the Michigan Mind

*Ferndale, Michigan, USA*

Dear Sherlock,

I have lost my mind and I don't know where to start looking for it. It is about four feet tall and four feet wide, and it is the smartest I ever had. So if you happen to see it, give me a call and I will give you part of it. You need it!

Sincerely yours,
        Norman Pinkoski

## The Drumstick Dilemma

*Toms River, New Jersey, USA*

Dear Sherlock Holmes,

I know that you are the greatest detective in the world. I lost one drumstick for my drum. And I wish that you would come here and find it for me. Thank you very much.

Owen Sweeney

## The Adventure of the Missing Quarter

*St Catherine's, Ontario, Canada*

Dear Sherlock Holmes,

I have a case I would like you to solve. It all started when I was in the library. I had a quarter and put it on the table. I turned round to get a book from the shelf and then turned back to get my quarter. It was gone! The only people who were around were the librarian, who was putting away books, and a boy who was two shelves away from me. I never found it, so I hope you can solve my problem.

Yours sincerely,
Donald Wininger

## The Bedminster Record

*Bedminster, New Jersey, USA*

Dear Mr Holmes,

A record was stolen from the music room of our school; date taken, September 26; date found missing, September 29. No clues, no suspects. Please solve this mystery.

Yours truly,
Steve Burd, Paul Potts

## Pippin Passes

*Westchester, Pennsylvania, USA*

Dear Sherlock Holmes,

Please help me! My cat Pippin was kidnapped (I should say catnapped), and she hasn't been found. I haven't been able to get my mind off her. She always used to wake me up at 6.30 for school. Now that she's gone, I can't seem to wake up.

Mr Holmes, I miss Pippin very much and I want you to help me find her. I know you won't let me down, so I'm counting on you. Please contact me as soon as you can. Thank you.

Sincerely,
Jennifer Haw

## The Case of Burschi, the Housecat

*Köln, West Germany*

Dear Mr Holmes,

I've got your address from a friend and I hope that you can help me. Two years ago disappears our housecat, Burschi. It had only one year stay with our family. What meaning thereby? She will be free, or has anybody her for catmeat?

Most respectful,
Silke

## The Three Black Cats

*Detroit, Michigan, USA*

Dear Mr Holmes,

Sir, the Problem of the Three Black Cats grows more difficult as each day passes. We are in need of your help.

Please reply as soon as possible. Thank you.

Awaiting your reply,
R. W. M. Lawler

## The Dog in the Night

*Kramfors, Sweden*

Dear Mr Holmes,

I need your help. I have a very queer dog. He behaves normally all day; he has small eyes, a short nose and a head like a tennis ball. But when evening comes, he's not like a dog any longer. He looks more like a monster. He runs away very quickly and comes home in the morning. I can hear when he comes, then I take my pillow and put it over my head so that I don't have to hear him.

Now, Mr Holmes, I just wanted you to help me to figure out what he's doing during the nights. Do you think this is normal for a little dog? I don't think so. So now I want you to take a train to my place. When you arrive, you just have to ask after me.

Yours sincerely,
Anna Lena Steen

## The Case of the Hazel Park Fish

*Hazel Park, Michigan, USA*

Dear Mr Holmes,

I would like you to solve the case of the Hazel Park fish: 'The fish was missing about an hour, then he was seen walking down the street with an alligator behind him. I started to run after him, but he flew away. I went home to sit down and the fish was standing there laughing.' Can you explain this?

Sincerely,
      Billy Wall

## The Uelzen Budgerigar

*Uelzen, West Germany*

Dear Mr Holmes,

I've got a big problem. I've had a budgie, but yesterday he flew away. I don't know what to do. Can you come and help me? Please write soon.

Yours,
Sven Kablau

## The Flight of the Parakeet

*Dayton, Ohio, USA*

Dear Sherlock,

I am in serious trouble. I came home the other night and went upstairs to my brother's parakeet cage. I wanted to give the bird some soup. This he ate and then flew away. I don't know what to do. My brother is away at school and his parakeet is about the only thing he comes home for. Please help me!

Kurt Laursen

## The Lion's Malady

*Rüsselsheim, West Germany*

Hey Sherlock!

I know you're the best. My lion is ill. What can I do? Please help me.

Yours,
Markus Weidner

# Thumper of Waterloo

Waterloo, Iowa, USA

Dear Mr Holmes and Dr Watson,

About two months ago my pet rabbit, Thumper, was taken from his cage. This happened while my family and I were asleep one Saturday night and we discovered him missing on Sunday morning after we came home from church.

You both will think that he just got out of his cage and ran away. That's not so. Thumper's cage was three feet off the ground and he was scared to jump that far because he was getting old. I used to take Thumper out of his cage every day and let him run loose and he would never leave the yard or alley. Also, on his cage I had an unlocked lock to keep little kids from opening it.

We could tell that Thumper put up a good fight because all of his food and water was thrown about. Also his hay was torn up. Thumper would have come home if he were alive. I know that somebody could have let him go someplace far away, but I have a feeling he's not alive.

I would feel so much better if you both would help me to find out who took Thumper. Everyone loved him and wants him back. So would you please help me out.

Thank you so much,

Ann Rotsaert

# The Tame Tarantula, the Helicopter and the Bananas

Vancouver, Canada

Dear Sherlock Holmes,

I have been reading your books with my tutor and I like them. My pet tarantula has been kidnapped; they want a helicopter full of bananas before they will send him back to me. Please help me.

Yours truly,

Robert Cohen

# The Squeaking Duck of Ernie

*Friedberg, West Germany*

Dear Mr Sherlock Holmes,

I would be glad if it's possible for you to help the German police in a very mysterious robbery. The robbery was told to the people in nearly every newspaper: the squeaking duck of Ernie is stolen!

I would like to have also an autogram card from you. I collect these things and your card is an important object for me beside the Queen of England and the President of Germany. Thanks.

Please write soon,
                    Suse Halbe

# [ 6 ]
# The Supernatural

## Re *Vampires*

*Cave Junction, Oregon, USA*

Dear Mr Holmes,

I was wondering if there were any real vampires. If there are, how do you keep them away from you?

Thank you,
Dave Sorensen

## *Vampirism in America*

*Cranston, Rhode Island, USA*

Dear Mr Holmes,

I am writing to you in the hope that you will help me in a rather unusual undertaking. This offer, which I am about to put forward for your consideration, involves a somewhat difficult and bizarre case of tracing; but I know of no better-qualified man – or detective that I admire more – than yourself. If you would, Mr Holmes, I'd like you to locate for me a 'living', preferably male, vampire.

Before you take this to be some kind of practical joke and throw it away, let me elaborate on my seemingly mad request. The study of vampirism has always been a fascinating one for me. Although not too many people care to involve themselves with this sort of subject, I have researched it extensively and through my laborious studies I have discovered that these marvellous beings exist!

So please, Mr Holmes, I beg you to think seriously about my offer.

I know that if I could show you the evidence I have collected, you too would be convinced – not only of the existence of vampires, but also of the deep sincerity with which I make my request.

Thank you very much, sir, in advance for your kind help and early reply.

Most sincerely yours,
Evelyn Green


## The Case of the Illinois Valley Vampires

*Cave Junction, Oregon*

Dear Mr Holmes,

We have a very important problem in the Illinois Valley. It seems that there are several wild vampires going around the valley. They are wild because they travel in the daylight. One day, one of our famous scientists, Dr Rigby, captured one of these vampires when it was on the loose. As he was examining it, the vampire opened one of its eyes and he saw a contact lens. This wasn't an ordinary lens, these lenses are sun-glasses. That explains why the vampires come out in the daylight instead of at night.

There is a $500 reward if anyone can find a way of capturing these vampires. I was hoping you could help me.

Sincerely yours,
Theresa Benson

## The German Horror

*Sulzbach-Rosenberg, West Germany*

Hello Mr Holmes!

In our house is a big monster with the name 'Dead Devil' living. Please help me. You must come as fast as you can to Sulzbach-Rosenberg in West Germany. Street: Kreuzenweg 9.

Your
    Jürgen Sandner


## Chimes at Midnight

*Meaford, Ontario, Canada*

Dear Sherlock Holmes,

I have a problem that needs to be solved. Every night at midnight a bell rings, but there is no bell in Meaford or in any of the nearby towns. We have been to the police, but they can't figure it out. If you have any advice, would you please enclose it in a letter.

Sincerely yours,
    Lynn Adams


## The Southaven Mystery

*Southaven, Mississippi, USA*

Dear Mr Holmes,

Mr Holmes, the reason for my writing is a series of incidents which occurred a fortnight ago and then again last night.

On December 26th, I was drowsily reading a book in the confinement of my study when all of a sudden there was a high pitched very shrill noise that sounded like a whistle. I looked and looked for the place it was coming from but, before I could locate the noise, it stopped. I thought it must have been the wind, but last night the same thing happened while I was in my bedroom and there was no wind at all.

Mr Holmes, I feel that there is something very mysterious going on and I would like to have your help. Please write back with an answer because I am scared desperate. Thank you.

Fondly,
    Don Williams

## The Texas Poltergeist

*Richardson, Texas, USA*

Dear Sherlock Holmes,

I'm so scared and frightened! For the last week our furniture has been rearranged while my family and I have been sleeping. There are no clues as to who is doing the re-arranging. Our doors and windows are locked at night, so no one can get in. There are no footprints or fingerprints on the furniture or anywhere in the house.

One time I stayed up all night. I didn't see anything, but I could hear the furniture being moved around. I've called the police and they came to the house to investigate the incident. After weeks of looking and snooping around the house, they gave up and left.

Please come; my family and I are petrified beyond belief. I don't make a lot of money, but I'll gladly pay you all I have.

Sincerely,
    Kevin Ryan

P.S. If you want to, you can bring Dr Watson with you.

# The Ghost of Bielefeld

*Bielefeld, West Germany*

Dear Mr Holmes,

I got your name and address from a girl friend of mine who read all your detective occurrences and she told me about your very successful works.

My special problems are curious noises in my room and in the corridor outside. I fear a ghost is existing and some people are believing that the ghost of our house has been there for three years now. It always makes its appearance five minutes past midnight.

Therefore I want advice from you what it is to do in that special situation?

With kind regards.

Yours sincerely,
Sonya Kleineberg

# The Austin Apparition

*Austin, Texas, USA*

Distinguished Mr Holmes,

I have just recently been informed of your existence in London. I trust that you will accept my most humble apologies for my previous ignorance of that fact. I was very grateful indeed to learn of your residence in England for I have a mystery with which I need some assistance. I will relate my story, and, if possible, please send any ideas or hints pertaining to the solution.

In Austin, Texas, there is a particular house which has a reputation for not being inhabited by anyone for more than a few weeks at a time. I frequently pass this house going to and from work and have been inside it once. I had never noticed anything unusual about this house until yesterday. As I drove past I saw a shadow moving rapidly across the front yard, but there was nothing there to cast the shadow. Furthermore, the shadow was being cast in the wrong direction for the sun's location. Also, the time that I was inside the house I felt an odd sensation as if I were shrinking. The landlord simply cannot keep the house rented continuously, so I am certain that these peculiarities are related to that fact in some way. As of yet I have been unable to reach a conclusion and would therefore be immeasurably thankful for any help you may be able to offer.

Thank you,
> Lynette Reed

## The Case of the Stolen Tombstone

*Braintree, Massachusetts, USA*

Dear Mr Holmes,

I need your help in solving a murder mystery. I call it 'The Stolen Tombstone'.

About five years ago an elderly woman by the name of Martha Hopkins died an evil death. She was stabbed eighty-seven times. The thing that puzzled me is that it happened on her eighty-seventh birthday.

Just recently her tombstone was stolen. By whom we have no idea. We don't think it was anyone she knew, and it couldn't have been the man who killed her because he had supposedly gone insane and died, or had he?

It happened on August 16th, during the night. One of the neighbours said that he heard something like metal banging against rock. He called the police, and as soon as they got there to see what was going on, they discovered that the tombstone was missing. But they couldn't find any clues or fingerprints and none of the rocks had been moved or jolted. They are still puzzled about this. Please try to solve it.

Sincerely,
> Kim Gersu

## The Arlington Toe-impression Scandal

*Arlington, Texas*

Dear Holmes,

Every time I go outside my window I see strange things. I see footprints
with three toes and blood on the house. Please come quick!

## The Great Pumpkin Hoax

*Ferndale, Michigan*

Dear Sherlock Holmes,

I wrote a letter to the Great Pumpkin and I told him that I have been
a good boy, because on Halloween night the Great Pumpkin rises out
of the pumpkin patch and gives presents to all the good little boys and
girls. I sent the letter, and on Halloween night I went to the pumpkin
patch and waited and waited. I waited all night but he never showed
up. For that I missed 'trick or treating'. Please help me to find out if
there is a Great Pumpkin or not.

Thank you,
Curt Young

## The Hunchback of Decatur

*Decatur, Illinois, USA*

Dear Mr Holmes,

I've read your stories and I like them alot, but I didn't believe them
until this happened to me. On a Monday night, a friend and I went up
to the club swimming-pool. As we walked through the woods, we saw
a man. He looked like the Hunchback of Notre Dame. Then we got up

closer. It was! Black hair, humpback, trench coat and just everything. He started chasing us and we cleared out.

I can't figure it out, it wasn't a member of my family. So, please, please try to help us. I'll pay your plane fee.

Sincerely yours,
Susan Emerson


## The Loch Ness Monster

*Boise, Idaho, USA*

Dear Sherlock,

I've been really interested in the Loch Ness monster. It has always been a mystery to me. Please write back and tell me what you think the Loch Ness monster is. Do you believe there really is a monster in that deep blue water?

Sincerely,
Jill Goes


## The Devil's Triangle Mystery

*Silver Spring, Maryland, USA*

Dear Mr Holmes,

My husband is a great admirer of yours and he is also very interested in the Devil's Triangle Mystery. Would you please crack the case especially for him and send him the solution.

I would appreciate it if you would reply before Christmas so that I can put your letter in his stocking for a happy surprise to him.

Sincerely,
Linda Keys

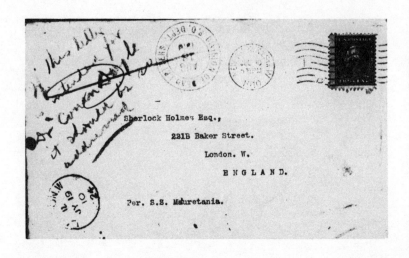

Sherlock Holmes Esq.,

221B Baker Street.

London. W.

E N G L A N D.

Per. S.S. Mauretania.

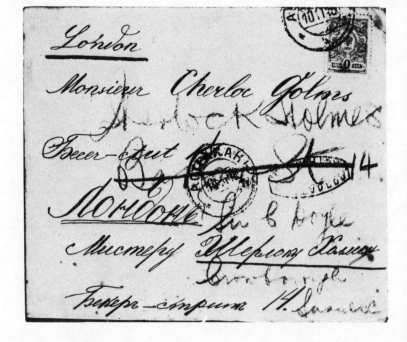

London

Monsieur Cherloc Golmes

Бекер-стрит

Лондон

Мистеру Шерлоку Холмс

Бекер-стрит 14. Лондон

# The Bermuda Triangle

*Boise, Idaho, USA*

Dear Mr Holmes,

A year or so ago I read in a magazine about the Bermuda Triangle. Ever since, I have wondered just how all of those ships and planes disappeared. Some people think beings from Outer Space are capturing them all, others think there is something at the bottom of the ocean that is taking them. I wanted to know what you think has happened to all of these ships and planes. Please write back and tell me your theory.

Sincerely,
> Deb Alter


# The Waitsfield Space Wonder

*Waitsfield, Vermont, USA*

Dear Mr Holmes,

Here in the USA, as well as all over the world, UFOs are flying around scaring people half to death. They are landing all over the place. People have taken pictures of them.

Could you find out if there are really UFOs or not? Do you think that the Bermuda Triangle is a mystery? Can you explain it? The world would love to know. Thank you.

Sincerely,
> Brian Kerr

# [ 7 ]
# Personal Problems and Riddles

## The Westchester Gum Bribe

*Westchester, Pennsylvania, USA*

Dear Mr Holmes,

My problem is that my brother always beats me up. I would like to know how to make him stop. I've told my friends and his friends to dislike him, but that never works. I even tried to bribe him, telling him if he would stop beating on me I would give him a pack of gum or a dollar bill. I hope you find an answer.

Sincerely,
            Todd Turbedsky

## The Derby Block Vandals

*Derby, Kansas, USA*

Mr Sherlock Holmes,

There is at least one case of vandalism every night on my block. My fourteen-year-old brother and I are getting the blame for it. I would like you to come to my block and solve my case. I will pay you $200 a week.

Yours truly,
            Mike Main

## The Goodwin Gang

*Ferndale, Michigan, USA*

I have a big problem. I hang around with a lot of girls. At school we are known as the Goodwin Gang. One day we got a letter that said obscene things about all of us; then we got more of them saying sickening things. We don't know who wrote them. That's why we need you. We will pay you $500 if you can find out who wrote the letters.

Sincerely yours,
Carol Nowak


## A Canadian Compromise

*Pembroke, Ontario, Canada*

Mr Holmes,

I am one of your many fans with a small problem, so I would appreciate it very much if you will answer my question. My school year is taking a turn for the worse and I am compromising on being a dropout. I would like your answer whether I should continue to make the way to drop out or try and make the best of my eleventh year.

Thank you,
Steve Brown


## The Gilbert Girl

*Gilbert, Arizona, USA*

Dear Mr Sherlock Holmes,

I'm twelve years old. Now that next year I'll be a teenager I hang around with a lot of girls and boys. Every girl I play with has a boyfriend, and when I ask someone to go with me they say no, because I'm too shy. What should I do?

Jo Ann Caballero


## The Cloud of Unknowing

*Springfield, Illinois, USA*

Dear Sherlock Holmes,

How are you supposed to find out if a boy likes you without coming straight out and asking him? I have had friends ask him, but I never get a true answer. He always says to them, 'What do you care,' or something like that. I am very shy around boys.

Sincerely yours,
Carla Trello


## The Vision of Anja

*Bielefeld, West Germany*

Dear Mr Holmes!

First I want to say that my English is often very faulty, but although this is a fact I think and hope that you can read and understand everything.

And now my problem: I have attempted of all kinds to get an autograph of Marc Almond (he's the singer of Soft Cell, an English group, and he is very good-looking so I like him) and every attempt remained vainly. I request you, Mr Holmes, to help me, a young girl who's total despairing, hope for the autograph of her vision of man, because my own possibilities are at an end.

So I have the favour to ask of you the autograph-address of Marc

Almond to come to know for me. I know that this is not a quite right event and I can't pay a fee for your answer, but I'm sure that you can nevertheless do something for me.

With many salutations,
Anja Girteit

## The Go-Between

*Wembley, Middlesex*

Dear Sherlock Holmes,

I write to you now, on a subject which is dear to my heart, but which, until I heard of your invaluable services, seemed to me to be utterly insurmountable.

The affair involves no less than a beautiful young lady of fine distinction, a pot of gold and the somewhat romantic whims of your humble servant.

The young lady in question has been receiving the attentions of the aforementioned gentleman, but has not yet been able to identify her suitor. In order to perpetuate this state of affairs, it has become necessary to establish a reputable, yet at the same time, mysterious go-between who can be trusted implicitly to withhold the identity of the undersigned party.

To this end, I will now ask you to pass on any such correspondence as might arrive from the lady, to the address at the top of this letter. Such correspondence will most probably be addressed simply to 'Sherlock' and will most probably bear the postmark of Highbury, Islington or thereabouts. The letter will be in the form of an enquiry as to the identity and motives of the above-mentioned personage.

I cannot stress enough the importance of secrecy and hasten to add that in due time, all will be revealed to the young lady. I humbly request your co-operation on this matter, dear to my heart, and apologize for any inconvenience on your part.

Your humble servant,
Richard

## The Mystery of the Telford Barker

*Telford, Shropshire*

Dear Sir,

My school-teacher said if I wrote to you I would get a reply. Anyway the thing I'm writing to you about is the mystery of the shouting school-teacher. I know it's daft but it's a mystery. I want to know why he shouts when he does not need to.

From
    Mark Kelsey

# The Story of the Man with the Watches

*Poole, Dorset*

Dear Sherlock,

Could you and Dr Watson put your amazing talents to work on this little mystery for me. I was watching TV on Wednesday, 3rd November when I saw something very unusual. A chap was on a show called ... Hmm, I can't remember. But I'm sure you can deduce it. Anyhow this chap was wearing two wrist-watches. Why do you think this was so? Is he a member of a secret society plotting against the Government? Is he a crank? Or does he wear them for some other sinister reason?

Yours faithfully,
L. Booth

# The Czech Interpreter

*Zilina, Czechoslovakia*

Dear Sir,

I send you a long letter from Czechoslovakia. I read an English newspaper, *Morning Star*, and I understand not the words: G.I. Joe, You Gotta Go – M.P.'s wife Joins No. 10 Vigil – TUC Leaders to Meet Chancellor – 8st Woman assaulted 17st P.C.

I was rather disappointed because my pocket dictionary proved to be of little use.

Please write to me if you know where are the words. I can't say how much I am looking forward to your reply.

With best wishes.

Yours sincerely,
Miroslav Petrak

# The Moon Tree Connection

*Windsor, Ontario, Canada*

Holmes,

No time. Shadows approach in the circumstance of the Moon Tree Connection. Find enclosed the last article. Reply at once.

MCHL

*The Last Article:*

---

# The Brazil Blackmail Conundrum

*Philadelphia, Pennsylvania, USA*

Dear Mr Holmes,

How are you doing? And how is Dr Watson? I have a mystery for you to solve. There lived a policeman and his son. One day the son was missing, and all the father saw was a note saying, 'I am in Brazil. Pay a ransom of $10,000'. How did the father know his son was not in Brazil? And how did he know that he was in the neighbourhood?

    Sincerely yours,

        Ernest Turner

## The Rugger Skipper's Riddle

*Trinity College, Cambridge*

Dear Holmes,

What is this?

$$\left.\begin{array}{cccccc} 1 & 2 & 3 & 6 & 9 & 7 \\ 6 & 3 & 7 & 8 & 2 & 1 \\ 0 & 0 & 1 & 2 & 0 & 1 \\ 5 & 5 & 0 & 0 & 5 & 5 \end{array}\right\}\pi$$

$$2\ 8$$

$$1\ 1 \qquad \text{etc.}$$

Yours sincerely,
        Cyril Overton

# [8]
## 221B Baker Street

### The Correct Address

*Bronx, New York, USA*

Dear Sir,

I am writing this to see if this is the correct address of the residence of Sherlock Holmes, consulting detective, and Dr Watson, his (your?) partner in solving crimes. Is it?

Sincerely,
Irving Peck

### Castles in Baker Street

*Lakeside, California, USA*

Dear Sherlock Holmes,

You are the best detective in the world. Do you live in a castle? And, if you do, what is it like? Thank you.

Sincerely,
Gregg Romano

## The Dartmouth Caller

*Dartmouth, Nova Scotia, Canada*

Dear Mr Sherlock Holmes,

In anticipation of the possibility that I may be in London in the very near future, I would like, sir, to request your permission to visit you at 221B Baker Street. I would be honoured if you would grant my request.

Yours truly,
Robin Reid


## An Odyssey from Ithaca

*Ithaca, New York, USA*

Dear Sherlock Holmes,

I am a reader of your adventures and, for that matter, a re-reader. I have often wondered what 221B Baker Street was like. We will be in London through the week of June 9th. We will be staying at Ebury Court Hotel, 26 Ebury Street, London, SW1. I would be thrilled if you would write to me at the above address and mark 'Hold for arrival', letting us know when it would be convenient to visit your rooms at Baker Street.

Sincerely,
Sarah Lambert

P.S. I'm twelve years old and will be travelling with a party of two parents.

The Hound of the
Baskervilles
The faithful Watson goes alone to
Dartmoor to help Holmes with
the problem of the ghostly and
gigantic hound that has caused
the death of more than one
Baskerville. But the hound proves
to be as vital as its burglaries and
Holmes, resolver at hand, arrives
in the nick of time to save the
latest quarry.

# A Thanksgiving Letter

*Erie, Pennsylvania, USA*

Dear Sherlock Holmes,

I was in England recently and I saw your house, but I didn't know you still lived there. Had I realized you were still in occupancy I would have stopped by. I am sorry I missed the opportunity of talking with you personally.

What interesting cases have you solved lately? Could you give me some helpful pointers on pursuing a career in detective work, please? This information would be greatly appreciated as I am thinking of following in your footsteps. Would it be possible for you to give me a short rundown of how you got started in this field?

I would also enjoy a picture of you and Dr Watson standing in front of your house, autographed if you would.

If you ever find yourself in Erie, Pennsylvania, working on a case, please feel free to use my home as your headquarters.

I am writing to you during the thanksgiving holiday season, thinking you will not be away on an assignment, therefore I will get a direct, personal reply from you.

Have a Happy Thanksgiving and give my regards to Dr Watson.

Sincerely,
Sarah Warthman


# The Doors of Detection

*Montreat, North Carolina, USA*

Dear Mr Sherlock Holmes,

The grandson we had with us for three weeks at the American Summer Institute at St Andrews, Scotland, in July, expressed a great desire to stand before 221B Baker Street when we visited London.

Certainly, such a desire needed fulfilment – and he speaks of this often. He will not forget this visit.

Hearing of your plan to send a memento to inquirers, I am requesting that in your good time you make some acknowledgement of this late afternoon visit on July 30. Any interesting sentence you send would be intriguing to our grandson.

Yours, with great appreciation,

Harry H. Bryan

## The Timoshenko Photographs

Jamaica, New York, USA

Dear Sirs,

Please send me a colour picture of the inside and outside of 221B Baker Street (and *all* of Mr Holmes's rooms).

Thank you,

Victor Timoshenko

P.S. And the negatives too, please!

## The Hude Zimmermann Plans

Hude, West Germany

Dear Sherlock Holmes!

I know you live in the past, but I am fascinated from your abilities.

A little while ago I bought the complete set of the original Sherlock Holmes adventures from Sir Arthur Conan Doyle. I read it more than one time.

Now my question. Is it, perhaps, possible to receive a floor plan of the residence of the great detective and an autogram from the same and his friend, Dr Watson?

Thank you very much in advance.

With kindly regards,
                    Johann Zimmermann


## 221A Baker Street

*Wantage, Berkshire*

Dear Sir,

I am curious to know whether or not there is a 221A Baker Street and, if so, whether it is at present vacant. I am seeking lodgings in the metropolis and can think of no address that would suit me better.

I would be indebted to you, Mr Holmes, if you would favour me with a reply, and I remain,

Ever truly yours,
                    John Rutherford


## The Great Hiatus

*London* W12

Dear Mr Holmes,

As a visitor to London I recently attended a walk called 'In the footsteps of Sherlock Holmes'. Although the guide pointed out many interesting places connected with your past cases, I was most disappointed to find that your rooms at 221B were undergoing repairs. Since you are probably staying at a hotel until the repairs are complete, it is unlikely that we shall be able to meet this time. However, let me wish you a happy new year and hope that we can meet another time.

Yours sincerely,
Sachiko Nakamura


## The Little Matter of the Sussex Furniture Van

*No fixed abode*

Dearest Mr Holmes,

I feared the worst when I was told that you had moved. Why did you leave your residence at 221B Baker Street?

I met Watson a few days ago in Belfast. Charming old chap! He told me they caught the 'ripper'. Is it so? Who is he?

The weather has been miserable these past few weeks and the wife has been giving me some trouble. However, life's been good.

Hope to hear from you soon,
Sir Jeremy Slate


## Mrs Hudson's New Lodgers

*Jordan, New York*

Dear Resident of 221B,

I am a fan of Sherlock Holmes and I am curious to know who lives at the house now. Please write back and tell me your name and what 221B Baker Street looks like nowadays.

Sincerely,
Marianna Fikes

# The Adventure of the Blackpool Builder

*Lytham St Annes, Near Blackpool, Lancashire*
Dear Mr Holmes,

My friend Mr Hatherley came to you following the loss of his thumb, what I have lost is a brick. You may smile, Mr Holmes, but such a minor object as this has caused me considerable worry.

Before my wife left for a visit to France, she ordered the building of a summer house. So important was it to her that it should be constructed to her personal requirements that she asked that each brick be numbered to ensure correct positioning. The 500 bricks were supplied by a company called Bates & Co., so naturally each brick was numbered and suffixed by the letter 'B', thus 1B, 2B, 3B, through to 500B. Alas, one brick has disappeared. I fear a spiteful bricknapper is the culprit.

Without this brick no further work can be done! I am afraid it will break my wife's heart if she returns to find the building incomplete. I hope you will let me know whether the brick has been found and if it can be returned to me; also what price, if any, I must pay.

Yours sincerely,
David Fisher

P.S. The missing brick by coincidence is No. 221B.


# The Bricks of London

*Bournemouth, Dorset*
Dear Sir,

I understand that one can purchase an old brick from the building of 221B Baker Street which is being renovated.

Please find enclosed a cheque for purchase of one brick from the above building. I enclose a stamped addressed envelope for a reply.

Yours faithfully,
Sheila Curry

## The Colossal Schemes of
## Master John Palmer

*Portsmouth, Hampshire*

Dear Sir,

Are you still selling the bricks from 221B Baker Street, as during the holidays? When I was in London I hoped to see Sherlock's residence, but only found a bank being erected on the site. Will there be any exhibits of Sherlock Holmes when that is completed?

I have lately put on a play to a host of people. It began with the shadow of Holmes on a sheet and then Holmes reading the daily paper. It ended with the explanation and clues, one of which was a skeleton key! The play was named *The Locked Room Mystery*. I am now making a film called *The Man with the Twisted Limp*, featuring a strange man pursuiting Holmes and Watson as they track down the Hinton Hound!

I hope one day to be a detective myself and join the C.I.D. With my Holmesian powers of deduction I'll stamp out villainy, including Moriarty!

Thank you, with every deduction,

John Palmer

## Baker Street Spa

*Stony Brook, New York, USA*

Dear Sir,

I am anxious to find out if you have any bricks left from the 221 building – also bottles of that precious water that was seeping up through the well in the basement. If so, please let me know the price and I will send a cheque by return mail.

Sincerely,

Helen Heinrich

# The Cobblestone Postscript

Allenstown, New Hampshire, USA

Dear Mr Holmes,

How do you feel? I just received the letter that you sent me. I found it very interesting and was wondering if you could send me a couple more pictures of your room. I was also wondering if you could send me a list of your ten favourite cases. I have just read your casebook and really enjoyed it.

I am hoping to get over to your wonderful country with the C.A.P. (Civil Air Patrol) this summer, and I would make it a point to come and see you. Goodbye for now.

Your No. 1 fan,

Alfred Desrochers

P.S. Could you send me a cobblestone from a London street?

# [ 9 ]
# Sherlockian Institutions

## The Baker Street Police Division

*College Park, Georgia, USA*

Mr Sherlock Holmes,

At the risk of seeming impertinent, Mr Holmes, may I ask that this epistle serve as an introduction by correspondence? Your fame as an analytical sleuth and devotee of the deductive method is widespread here in the colonies and I have avidly followed Dr Watson's accounts of your investigations.

Delving at the heart of the matter, sir, I should like to apply for a position as a member of the Baker Street Irregulars. I have all the makings of a fine street arab and am particularly proficient at eavesdropping, rumour-mongering, pocket-picking, cursing and general low behaviour.

If you can find an opening in the irregular organization, I shall be honoured to serve in any capacity. Thank you for your consideration. Regards to the good doctor.

Respectfully yours,

James E. Curtin


## The Sherlock Holmes
## Admiration Society

*Clanfield, Hampshire*

Dear Sir,

I understand that a society has been formed in your honour and I should be indebted to you if you would put me in contact with it.

May I take this opportunity of expressing my great admiration for you and your work. Your efforts at bringing justice to many a machiavellian plot deserve the utmost praise.

I am, dear Sir, Yours faithfully,

R. T. Matthews

## The Sherlock Holmes Society

*Balliol College, Oxford*

Dear Sir,

Ever since I was a small child I have enjoyed all and everything to do with Sherlock Holmes – although mainly, of course, the stories. I pride myself on the detailed knowledge I have of many of the short stories and of *The Hound of the Baskervilles*.

I am under no delusions as to the 'existence' of Sherlock Holmes as some people who write to your address seem to be – I *know* he exists (in spirit if not in body!).

I wonder if you could possibly forward me any details of the Sherlock Holmes Society, with a view to my joining?

Thank you for your anticipated co-operation.

Yours truly,

N. Stuart

## The International Union of Associated Holmes Societies

*Bolingbrook, Illinois, USA*

To whom it may concern,

I do realize that Mr Sherlock Holmes no longer resides at 221B Baker Street and if I had indeed intended to correspond with him I should have addressed this to Sussex where he is caring for his bees and perhaps compiling the information for the book on crime detection that he has planned so long to write.

I am writing to receive some information on the Sherlock Holmes Society of London and its fellow organization, The Baker Street Irregulars, in New York. Of the first I would particularly like to know about the *Sherlock Holmes Journal*, and of the latter, an address at which I may contact that august society.

Many thanks for all help and the pleasure I have received sending a missive to that well-known address.

Linda de Viney


## The Sherlock Holmes Estate

*Costa Mesa, California, USA*

Dear Sir,

I am addressing this letter to the 'Estate of Sherlock Holmes' for want of a more accurate address. I would appreciate it very much if you would give me a list of the addresses of a few of the societies dedicated to the study of the Sherlock Holmes stories. To my amazement none are listed in the Los Angeles phone directory. Also, if you still have available photographs of the detective's Baker Street sitting-room, I'd very much like to have a few. Thank you very much.

Cordially,
Henry J. Vester III

# The Sherlockological Federation

*Jupiter Inlet Colony, Florida, USA*

Mr Holmes,

I am inquiring about the nearest organization devoted to yourself. I might also comment that I am extremely interested in the science of sherlockology. Thank you, and give my regards to Dr Watson.

Very sincerely yours,
Benjamin Clark Watson

# The Institute for the Advancement of Sherlockian Studies

*University of California, Riverside, California, USA*

Dear Mr Holmes,

First of all let me express my deep admiration and respect for your many exploits, adventures and services to man and state. I have been a follower and admirer of yours for several years now. And now I too, like so many others, am writing to you on a matter of 'professional business', although I fear that this is not a case to try your powers. I have been searching, without success, for the address of the Sherlock Holmes Society, either in London or preferably in America. Perhaps you have this bit of information in your index. If so, I would be most grateful if you could pass it along.

One other question, do you think the world is prepared for the story of the Giant Rat of Sumatra? Pray give my best to the good doctor and to Mrs Hudson. I remain,

Cordially yours,
Robert E. Bell

P.S. As a student of chemistry, I can only hope that my knowledge will one day be as 'profound' as yours.

## The Maiwand Veterans' Society

*Leighton Buzzard, Bedfordshire*

Dear Mr Holmes,

I would be most grateful if you could let me know the address – if you have it – of the American Scion Society of the Baker Street Irregulars called the Maiwand Jezails, as they recently issued a special stamp to commemorate the centenary of the battle of Maiwand in which Dr Watson was wounded. I appreciate the many calls on your time, so please just write the address overleaf, should you have it, and post in the enclosed stamped addressed envelope.

With very best wishes,

Ted Herbert

Victorian
Military Society


## *The Abbey Drugstore*
## *Sherlock Holmes Society*

*Universidad Pontificia Bolivariana,*
*Medellin, Colombia*

Gentlemen,

I am a Sherlock Holmes admirer and I would like to obtain information about your society activities and membership to the society.

Besides I am interested to buy the complete collection of Sherlock Book, that will include London and England maps of that time, and also a pipe as described in the books. I will greatly appreciate if you can send to me this information or at least the address of the place I can write in order to ask for it. Please forward all mail by AIR MAIL.

Cordially,

Eduardo Padilla Navas

## The Sherlock Holmes Association

*Brighton, Sussex*

Dear Sir,

Would you please send me information about your Sherlock Holmes association. I am sorry to have sent this to the wrong address, but I couldn't find the correct one.

Yours faithfully,

J. A. Rogers

## The Fan Club for Sherlock Holmes

*Bonn, West Germany*

Dear Sir,

It is a privilege for me to write you this letter, letting you know the intention of our class to organize the Sherlock Holmes Fan Club in our school.

We would be delighted to receive suggestions in this respect from you. Hoping to hear from you soon, I remain,

Yours respectfully,

Sebastian Balta

## The Holmes Club

*Baltimore, Maryland*

Dear Holmes Club,

I'd like to ask you: How does Sherlock Holmes deduce his deductions?

Thank you very much,

Barry Michaelson

## The Office of Sherlock Holmes and Dr Watson

*Park City, Illinois, USA*

Dear Sir,

Your assistance is requested in order to stimulate a young twelve-year-old into the enjoyment of being an armchair adventurer while reading about your famous cases and adventures.

It is respectfully requested that you send a reply to him personally. Such a letter from your offices and signed either by yourself or Dr Watson together with a recommendation as to which case to start with, should be a sufficient stimulus to produce results that will last his lifetime.

Thank you,
David L. Boswell

## The Holmes Poster Company

*London* W12

Dear Sir,

Please could you tell me where I could get pin-up posters of Sherlock Holmes. Also could you please tell me how to join the Sherlock Holmes fan club.

Yours,
Alan O'Brian

# Lodge 22½, New York

New York City, New York, USA

Mr Sherlock Holmes,

As a small tribute to the greatest detective of all time, I am about to start a Sherlock Holmes Club so that your name will always be known and honoured by many, many persons who have heard of you, read everything they can find about your wonderful life and wish to pass this knowledge on to a future generation. I am therefore asking you to send me some small token fron 22½ Baker Street to show my many friends, your friends and admirers. Just a small note to say you got this letter would be sufficient. Thank you very much indeed.

Very respectfully yours,

Mary Kennedy


# The Baker Street League

Halifax County, Nova Scotia, Canada

Dear Sir,

I recently found out that a fan club exists at the residence described by Doyle in his book about Sherlock Holmes. Finding this out, there are several questions I would like to ask about the author and his marvellous fictional creation.

The first question I will ask regards information on the 1959 movie version of *The Hound of the Baskervilles* which starred Peter Cushing and Christopher Lee. Someone told me that the movie was filmed on Sir Doyle's own estate. I was wondering if this is a false statement?

The second question I would like to ask is if Doyle had studied chemistry and utilized this knowledge into one of Holmes's talents, or did he receive information from people in the chemistry profession?

I have heard that the Chinese police-force training requires that Sherlock Holmes stories are to be read as a prerequisite to actual duty; I would like to know if this is true.

The final question is if Doyle wrote any other stories besides the Sherlock Holmes collection.

Tom Myers

## Club Sherlock Holmes

*Sienkiewicza, Poland*

Dear Madam or Sir!

Here in Poland we have heard a lot about Sherlock Holmes, also I have seen many films. I am very interested in him and I have heard that there is a club, which I should like to join.

Please be so kind as to send me full particulars. If it is not possible perhaps you could send me photographs.

Thanking you,
Andreis Janicki

## The Sherlock Holmes Club of London

*Heist-op-den-Berg, Belgium*

Dear Sir,

I hope you don't mind me addressing this letter to you personally, but I've been looking for the address of the 'Sherlock Holmes Club' in London for over one year now. I even asked the British Embassy in Brussels, but they didn't answer at all!

I know this isn't a case of criminality, but I would be helped a lot if you could procure me this address.

Send greetings to your companion and biographer, Dr Watson.

Sincerely,
De Haes Dirk

# The Sherlock Holmes
# Appreciation Society

*Middlesbrough, Cleveland*

Dear Sir,

I was recently informed that there was a 'Sherlock Holmes Appreci-ation Society' and that somebody is employed to answer any mail directed to his address.

As I have a sister who is deeply interested in anything to do with Mr Holmes, I wonder if you could send me any further details of the service you provide, to enable me to introduce her (so to speak). Please reply soon as I have Christmas in mind!

Yours faithfully,
Janice Robertson

## The Factory of Tobacco-Pipes

*Katowice, Poland*

Dear Sirs,

Please be so kind to let me have some labels of your Factory of Tobacco-pipes (or folders or the trade-mark of your Firm), because I am very interested with your products and I have much heard about your Factory of Tobacco-pipes.

Thanking you in anticipation and apologizing for the trouble caused, I remain,

Yours faithfully,
Lot Henryk

# [ 10 ]
## Letters about the Letters

### Sherlock Holmes
### to his Secretary

*Roslyn, Long Island, USA*

Dear Sir,

I am happy to see that you have replaced dear old Watson. My violin playing was too much for him. He deplores all forms of violins.

Just recently I was informed that my address is fictitious, a figment of Arthur Conan Doyle's imagination, and that I am non-existent. If this is true, then disregard this letter and those of anyone else inquiring about me. That dastardly fiend, Moriarty, is up to his old tricks again!

If by any chance you intend to follow in my footsteps, you will need to know something. I do have a case for you and I could send you a fine law suit.

By now, I hope you understand why I don't write my own memoirs. Fortunately my latest episodes have been chronicled. They are, 'The case of the Shattered Jigsaw', 'Monkey Business' and, of course, 'A Work of Art'.

Sherlock Holmes

### The Letter of Mrs Emonnet

*Le Pellerin, France*

Dear Sir,

I'm an English teacher in a French secondary school and I'm very anxious to know if you still employ a secretary to reply to Mr Sherlock

Holmes's mail. My pupils and I have recently read a text about that and, of course, we would like to check if that incredible but amusing detail is true.

I hope you will be so kind as to give us an answer. Any sort of documents concerning Mr Holmes would be very welcome.

Hoping to hear from you very soon,

Yours sincerely,
                                        Mrs Emonnet


## The Returned Cover Request

                                        *Brooklyn, New York, USA*
Dear Sir,

I was reading an article in the *New York Post* about letters that are written to Sherlock Holmes and Dr Watson. It is said that each letter is answered individually. I think this is very nice. I was wondering if you could send me a letter from 'Sherlock Holmes'. Could you also please enclose the envelope this letter came in. I want the cancelled envelope for a souvenir. Also, if there is any other souvenir material could you please enclose that.

Thank you very much,
                                        Steven Machover


## In Praise of the Abbey National

                                        *Appleton, Wisconsin, USA*
Dear Sir,

I am enclosing an article that appeared in our local newspaper not long ago. It so intrigued me that I was forced to cut it out and I was determined to write you.

I have read very few of Conan Doyle's works, being more inclined toward Agatha Christie myself. Nevertheless I am amazed at the number of gullible Americans who believe that Sherlock Holmes is a real person. In any case, had he ever been real, he would surely be dead by now.

I find it admirable and most commendable that the Abbey National Building Society employs you to answer all the letters addressed to Sherlock Holmes. It shows a great deal of respect for the common man and is certainly a good public-relations measure. I have nothing but praise for you and your company. May God grant you all the blessings you have so richly deserved.

With all my best wishes,
Kathryn Kleinhaus

## The Crazy Tie-Needle Conundrum

*Stade, West Germany*

Dear 'Mr Holmes'!

I read in a magazine about you and your work. I saw in the report a few letters of people who are write to you. First I didn't believe what they had written to you! What a nonsense! For example, a man writes he had lost his tie-needle and Sherlock must find it! Poor Sherlock Holmes! Is it really true that those people have written such letters? I can't understand that grown-ups can be able to so behave themselves like a child! And that they guess 'Mr Holmes' live! You must become crazy when you read such letters, or not? I get train if I read such ones!

Your
Gabi Stindt

# The Answered Correspondence

Dear Sir,

I have just read an article about you in the *Saturday Review of the Arts*. Getting a letter in reply was an interesting idea, and since I am a Holmes fan, a letter from him would be a real treat. So nice of you to answer his mail since he and Dr Watson are always so busy hunting down desperate crooks in so many books and throughout the world.

My favourite of all the stories of Mr Holmes is *The Hound of the Baskervilles* – a real chiller!

Please send me the photo and booklet about Mr Holmes, as I am anxious to have them for my collection of unusual letters and postcards. Until then, may I remain,

Respectfully,

# The Return of Dr Watson

Mineola, New York, USA

Dear Sir,

I am writing to you on behalf of my English teacher and class. We read an article on Sherlock Holmes and saw the address, and the class chose me to write to you requesting some information.

One of the questions that was brought up in our discussion was whether or not Dr Watson was killed in one of Sir Arthur Conan Doyle's books and was then brought back to life in his following book?

Another question was, while everybody knows that Sherlock Holmes is fictional, how do you, the person who is answering this letter, feel about it? Does he seem real to you, or just fictional?

We would appreciate any free material you could send us concerning Sherlock and anybody involved with him.

Thank you very much for reading this, and we all hope to hear from you soon.

Sincerely yours,
Terry Dias

## The Personal Private Secretary

West Linn, Oregon, USA

Sir/Madam,

I am aware that the famous and singular, professional but unofficial detective, Sherlock Holmes, and his trusted and devoted assistant, Dr Watson, no longer live at this address, and that the address in fact no longer exists. But, the reason I am writing is to confirm the reports that the mail of these two celebrated individuals continues to arrive at a rate that requires full-time personnel, supplied by the government, to process.

If this letter is read by someone other than Sherlock Holmes: Who, why? Please take a few minutes to answer these questions. What has become of Holmes, Watson and Doyle the literary agent? What is done with their mail?

Your immediate attention would be very much appreciated.

Thanking you in advance,
Kenneth S. Latham

## The Lady at Baker Street

Windom, Minnesota, USA

Dear Mr Sherlock Holmes,

I have read some of your detective stories and I think they are very interesting, especially at the end when you solve the mystery.

I know that all the letters sent to Sherlock Holmes are sent to a lady but I can't remember your name, so I'll just call you Sherlock.

When I heard that all the letters went to you and that you answered them, I became very interested and decided to write and find out if it is true. If it is, how can you answer so many letters without getting bored?

I have some further questions to ask you. Do you really enjoy your work? How many letters do you get a month? How long have you been doing this work? When the people who believe in Holmes ask you to come and solve their mysteries, what do you tell them? How did you get picked to answer Sherlock Holmes's letters?

Well, I hope you can answer these questions. I know you have millions of letters to write, but try to reply as soon as you can.

Very sincerely,
Lina Reha

## The St Petersburg Memorandum

St Petersburg, Florida, USA

Dear Madam,

I was informed of your strange position by a series of newspaper articles on your 'employer'. It must be a strange feeling indeed to be secretary to a fictional character, especially one as famous as Sherlock Holmes.

Included in one article was a sentence pertaining to the origins of letters to your 'employer'. It is my sincere wish that you and myself might correspond about the substance of the letters to Holmes.

Sincerely yours,
Jeremiah Hennessy

The traditional home of Sherlock Holmes, No 111, Baker Street, W. London

# A Message from
## the Union of Soviet Sherlockian Republics

*Chapligin, Lipetskaya Region, USSR*

Dear Madam,

I was very interested in the article in our Soviet newspaper *Komsomol-skaya Pravda*, in which I have read about my favourite hero – Mr Sherlock Holmes – and your work as his secretary.

You know, of course, that almost all our people, young and old, are fond of the stories by Sir A. Conan Doyle. But it's very difficult to find these stories in our shops, because there are so many readers of Conan Doyle.

I have some stories by this author in English. You see, I like them very much.

Be so kind as to write me some words about your work. I hope you will write me soon.

Yours truly,
        Ravitcheva Svetlana


## The Answering Service and the Press

*Columbia, Missouri, USA*

Dear Sherlock,

I am a reporter for the Columbia *Missourian*. I've heard about your answering service and would like to do a story on it. I would appreciate it if you would answer my questions.

First of all, who are you? When did you start on the job, and who pays you?

How many letters do you get? What kind of people write, and what do they say? Do you have any odd or interesting examples?

Finally, if you have any pictures available, either of yourself or of the apartment, I would be grateful for a copy. I know you must have a large work-load, but I would like to have the information as soon as possible.

Thank you,
> Steven Schrader

## The Letters of Mr Sherlock Holmes

*Montgomery, Alabama, USA*

Hello!

Recently, my family – residents of Montgomery, Alabama – visited friends in Jacksonville, Florida. These friends have collected countless tabloids and among them I discovered an old issue of the *National Enquirer* which carried the headline 'Sherlock Holmes still receives Fan Letters'. The article went on to say that a twenty-two-year-old secretary answered the letters to Sherlock Holmes, and she thought it surprising that 'many of them believe he is an actual person', and that 'many people seriously want him to solve cases for them'.

I, a freelance writer and reporter, found her comments most interesting – and I would like to up-date that article in the hopes of getting it published in a local magazine. To do this I need, of course, more information: How many letters, if any, still come in for Sherlock Holmes? If possible, could you inform me of several 'cases' he's been asked to solve? The name and age of the person who answers the letters today, and that person's comments on the overall aspect of the letters – problems arising from this accumulation (if any), the most amusing letters you've received and, last but not least, has the number of people increased or decreased as more of the Sherlock Holmes stories are made available to the reading public?

I would very much appreciate your help in this matter and would be glad to include any message from you to Mr Holmes's fans that you wish to have published.

I shall be most anxiously awaiting your answer on the subject of 'Mr Sherlock Holmes's Letters'.

Thank you,
> R. Anthony Pearcey

# The Collected Correspondence
## of a Consulting Detective

*Saratoga, California, USA*

Dear Madam,

I have heard that letters are sent to you from around the world in search of advice from Sherlock Holmes. After learning this, an idea popped into my head and I would like to share it with you. My idea is this. I would like to buy from you, for a price that you feel is reasonable, all the letters that have over the years been sent to you and addressed to Mr Sherlock Holmes.

I am extremely interested in Sherlock Holmes and I think it would be fun to put together such a collection of letters.

Please let me know if this would be possible.

Thank you,

Mike Oliver

## The Australian Lager Offer

*Darling Point, New South Wales, Australia*

Dear Madam,

It is about a year since we have been in communication. I have since read *The Seven-Per-Cent Solution* which was serialized in the *Sydney Morning Herald* and then published in hardback by Hodder and Stoughton. I think this book is excellent in every way, and with the parting between Sherlock Holmes and Dr Watson at Milan, with Watson to return to that extraordinarily nice wife of his and Holmes to commune with himself following the cure of his cocaine addiction by Dr Sigmund Freud, the way is left well and truly open for the next event.

I have been greatly intrigued by the way the Abbey National Building Society has organized the continuity of this extraordinary business. I hope you keep it up, and I hope that you get the support of publishers. Did your people have anything to do with the publication of Nicholas Meyer's book? And another thing, who pays for the upkeep of Baker Street? It's all very interesting.

Will you write me a little note and tell me if you drink beer, or anything that you want to write about? If you do drink beer, then when I send a crate of a Melbourne product called Fosters beer to certain business friends in London, I will send a similar thing to you.

Yours sincerely,
William J. Stack

## The Romantic Misadventure of a Dane

Harsens, Denmark

Dear Madam,

Or I don't know if I have to say 'Mr Sherlock Holmes'! It's so funny, for one hour ago I looked your picture up in a weekpaper, and I was reading that very interesting article about your double life as Mr Holmes, and I was thinking that it could be funny to write to you. This is what I am doing now.

You look very lovely in the picture, so I wonder, tell me, is there no one who is writing to you in your own name, or am I the first?

Well, let's stop here. Let me tell you a little about myself. I am a twenty-two-year-old Danish sailor with blue eyes and dark brown hair just a little over my ears. I am in charter between Skagen, Denmark, and Ullapool, Scotland, and I will be sailing this trip until about the first of April; then I think we will be going around Antwerp, London and Boston.

I had always been thinking that it would be lovely to write to an English girl, so if you don't mind, so good. I can see on your picture that you have no rings and if there is coming a day when you have nothing to do, then just come on and write to me.

Your friend,
Knud Aage Haj

# The East London Philatelist

*East London, Republic of South Africa*

Dear Sir,

The enclosed cutting from the *Daily Despatch*, East London, will perhaps partly explain my audacity in writing to you. It would appear that you receive letters from all over the world.

I started twelve months ago to collect used postage stamps and I have asked various people who handle incoming mail to cut off the portion of the envelopes with stamps (without causing damage to the perforations) and to forward them to me. Otherwise many beautiful stamps end up in trash cans which could have found a home in someone's album and have been kept for years, giving pleasure to many people.

I am only interested in receiving surplus stamps in order to help others. It is, in other words, a non-profit pastime. Please let me know if you could help me. Meanwhile, I remain,

Yours sincerely,

Robert Waddington

# How Mr Holmes's Secretaries Replied

Is Mr Holmes well? *Both he and Dr Watson are in the best of spirits.*

Did he have an enjoyable Christmas? *He has asked me to tell you that he had a very good Christmas.*

Would you wish him a Happy New Year? *Mr Holmes thanks you for your kind wishes and also wishes you a Happy New Year!*

Did Holmes have Red Indian blood? *No. He was born British and will always remain so.*

Is it true that Holmes has two children? *He has asked me to tell you that the story that he has two children is certainly not true. He is very surprised to hear about it!*

Does he use the telephone? *He certainly uses the telephone now that he has retired.*

Could Mr Holmes supply a copy of his monograph on tobacco ash? *Unfortunately Mr Holmes has mislaid the monograph on cigar and cigarette ashes and therefore is unable to help you.*

Does he have a spare copy of *The Hound of the Baskervilles*? *I regret that Mr Holmes does not keep copies of the novels written about him and is therefore unable to send you a copy of* The Hound of the Baskervilles.

Will Mr Holmes write any more books? *He has now retired from active detection work so it is unlikely that he will write any more books.*

Is *The Seven-Per-Cent Solution* authentic? *Mr Holmes asked me to write to you with the information that* The Seven-Per-Cent Solution *is based on other stories and thus is authentic in one sense.*

Would it be possible to have a recent photograph of Holmes and Watson? *I am unable to send you a photo of Dr Watson and Mr Holmes as they do not allow them to be taken as it could be dangerous.*

Can one buy the same tobacco that he smokes? *No. The brand used by Sherlock Holmes is specially produced for him alone.*

What did it cost in the 1890s? *He is unable to remember what price it was.*

Does Mr Holmes know where one can buy deer stalkers? *Mr Holmes has not bought any more hats recently so does not know where you might be able to buy one.*

What is the registration number of his car? *He has asked me to write and tell you that he does not in fact have a car.*

Does Holmes find it exciting being a detective? *He tells me that he finds being a detective very ordinary.*

Does Holmes operate alone or with other detectives? *He tends to operate alone and does not know many other detectives, either male or female.*

Has he ever been scared? *Mr Holmes has indeed been scared on some of his more dangerous cases.*

Do other people appreciate the risks Holmes takes and are they not greater than those faced by other detectives? *Mr Holmes was very pleased that you appreciate the dangers and problems that he experiences in his cases. Many of them are indeed dangerous and this is not always appreciated by many people. He feels that there are many other detectives doing equally good jobs but they are not often heard of. He is lucky to have had the publicity.*

Which was his favourite case? *Mr Holmes tells me that he enjoyed all the cases and does not have any special favourites.*

Was Watson a woman? *Mr Holmes has asked me to write and tell you that Dr Watson was certainly not a woman. Indeed he was married to a lady named Mary.*

Was he fat or thin? *On the question of Dr Watson's size, I believe that he was neither fat nor thin, but of medium build.*

Does Mr Holmes know if Moriarty is still alive? *He has asked me to tell you that Professor Moriarty is no longer alive.*

What was Moriarty's Christian name? *Mr Holmes has asked me to tell you that Professor Moriarty's first name was James.*

Why was Mycroft Holmes involved in so few cases? *Mr Holmes tells me that Mycroft was involved in only a few cases because he was not very interested in the art of detection.*

Was Mrs Hudson involved in any mysteries? *Mrs Hudson was not involved in any mysteries – she was just his housekeeper.*

Would Mr Holmes be able to come to America and give a talk? *I regret that, whilst Mr Holmes would be very pleased to come to your school and talk to you all, his diary is so full that I am unable to fit you in.*

Did Holmes ever investigate any of the murders committed by Jack

AT THIS PLACE NEW YEARS DAY, 1881
WERE SPOKEN THESE DEATHLESS WORDS

"YOU HAVE BEEN
IN AFGHANISTAN, I PERCEIVE."

BY

Mr. SHERLOCK HOLMES

IN GREETING TO

JOHN H. WATSON. M.D.

AT THEIR FIRST MEETING

THE BAKER STREET IRREGULARS ~ 1953
BY THE AMATEUR MENDICANTS AT THE CARCUS CLUB.

the Ripper? *Mr Holmes was never called in to investigate any of the cases.*

Has Holmes been called in to investigate the recent art thefts in Europe? *He has asked me to tell you that he is now retired and thus has not been called in on the art thefts.*

Does Mr Holmes believe in vampires? *No. He is certain that they do not exist. He has seen no evidence at all to change his mind on this.*

What are his views on Unidentified Flying Objects? *He feels that most occurrences can be easily explained as aircraft or a trick of the light.*

What does he think of the Bermuda triangle? *He does not think much of the Bermuda Triangle mystery.*

Can Mr Holmes suggest how a girl might find out if a boy likes her? *Mr Holmes thinks you will have to ask the boy outright.*

Would it be possible to call in at 221B sometime next month? *Unfortunately, Mr Holmes will be away for the next few months and will thus be unable to see you.*

Is there a Sherlock Holmes Fan Club at 221B Baker Street? *There is in fact no such club at this address, but you could try contacting the Sherlock Holmes Society of London at 8 Southern Road, Fortis Green, London N2 9LE.*

Is Sherlock Holmes part of a pipe factory? *Sherlock Holmes is not part of a tobacco and pipe firm. He was, however, a great pipe smoker.*

Is his secretary in charge of his affairs? *Whilst I reply to letters addressed to Sherlock Holmes, I regret that I am not solely in charge of his affairs.*

How many letters does Holmes receive, where are they from, and what do they say? *Sherlock Holmes receives approximately 700 letters a year from all over the world from such far-flung places as Australia, Indonesia, Czechoslovakia, Norway and, of course, the United States of America. He has been asked to solve a number of cases, including Watergate and the energy crisis. Some people offer him a fee, together with his passage paid to whichever country they are in, to solve some mystery surrounding them. The cases vary from solving the mystery of a cat's disappearance to solving gruesome murders.*

Does Sherlock Holmes have a worldwide following? *I would say that the number of Sherlock Holmes fans is on the increase and he really does enjoy a worldwide appeal.*

Was the *New York Post* right in saying that every letter is answered individually? *The article in the* New York Post *was indeed correct – I try and answer every letter individually.*

Would it be possible for Mr Holmes to reply personally? *Unfortunately, Mr Holmes is away at present investigating another mysterious case and so is unable to reply to you personally.*

Would it not be a good idea to publish some of the letters addressed to Mr Holmes? *Your idea has in fact been raised by several people. However, at present it is not our policy to publish the letters. It may at some time in the future be thought worthwhile to go ahead with this but unfortunately, I have to decline your offer at the moment.*